THEY WERE BOTH HIS CREATURES: FIRST, VIKTOR, THE GROTESQUE MONSTER, THEN EVA, THE EXQUISITE BRIDE. . . .

"I will not obey you! I will not!" Eva cried.

"You insult me—and I will not have it," Charles responded.

"You won't have it! You lied to me—and *you* are insulted? Who do you think you are?"

Charles looked so angry that for a moment Eva thought he would strike her. But he calmed abruptly, rocked back on his heels, folded his arms across his chest, and smiled.

"If you go on like this," he said, "I shall have to tell you." He spoke with a hint of menace, yet also with anticipation, and Eva took up the challenge.

"Tell me, then! I have a life of my own! You taught me, out of books—but you didn't *create* me! You didn't create *me!*"

Charles Frankenstein laughed. The sound chilled Eva more deeply than the coldest of winds.

"As a matter of fact, my dear," he said, savoring each word, "I did."

THE
BRIDE

VONDA N. McINTYRE

based on the screenplay by
LLOYD FONVIELLE

A DELL BOOK

Published by
Dell Publishing Co., Inc.
1 Dag Hammarskjold Plaza
New York, New York 10017

Dell ® TM 681510, Dell Publishing Co., Inc.

ISBN: 0-440-10801-2

Printed in the United States of America
First Dell printing—July 1985

Chapter 1

A flash of lightning, sudden, brilliant, illuminated the world more vividly and more intensely than sunlight on the clearest day. The moment of brightness turned the night's black rain to shards of silver. Thunder followed in an instant: the sharp *crack* of the lightning's touch upon the rocky ground, and the long rolling roar that caused the air and the earth to shudder and quake. Even the castle's massive granite walls trembled.

The heady storm-scent quickened Charles Frankenstein's excitement. He felt as if he balanced on the knife-edge of nature's fury, as if any misstep would send him plunging down the immense cliff of his ambition. Yet his exultation glowed so brightly as to cause even terror to pale, just as a blaze of lightning overwhelmed a candle's flickering spark.

Charles blinked against the afterimage of the lightning and turned away from the unglazed window. Shadow and substance melded, and his universe contracted until nothing existed but the dark stone room in which he stood: the room, and the seen and unseen beings within it.

Beyond the afterimage, sitting at the table in the center of the room, Dr. Zahlus played a desultory game of solitaire, cheating casually, sipping wine from a jeweled goblet. In his anticipation, in his excitement, Charles had almost forgotten the presence of his associate, his self-appointed mentor.

The afterimage faded. Yet still Charles perceived a sort of electric tension, as if the aether could not hold all the energy flowing through it, and so must spill some out. Charles felt as if his fine, pale hair must be standing away from his head, like a halo.

A halo? he thought. I wonder . . . Did Lucifer retain his halo, after his grasp for power, after his fall from grace?

The wind streamed in like a frigid river, carrying the chill scent of glacial ice and mountains. Charles shivered. The candle guttered and nearly died. Its flickering cast trembling light into even the most deeply shadowed recess of the circular chamber, where a powerful figure sat hunched and hidden.

The creature stared at him. Charles wondered that its eyes did not reflect the light like an animal's. But of course, in a manner of speaking, the creature's eyes were as human as any natural man's. This Charles knew as certainly as he knew the origin of the creature's every other organ, bone, muscle, and sinew.

Almost simultaneously, the next lightning bolt and thunder peal assaulted his senses. In the glare of white light the creature looked upon Charles with a penetrating stare, and Charles fancied that the creature's eyes were pleading with him, demanding of him that he complete his work. If it were true, that his spells had finally called up daemons and spirits, then this daemon did not obey. It compelled.

And it watched, and it waited.

Again the candle provided the only illumination; again, deep shadows hid the creature. It was as if, by some black art, he had disguised himself as granite. And perhaps that was not so farfetched, for the creature resembled some great pagan war-god, carved from stone to preside over idolatrous ceremonies.

As the heart of the thunderstorm approached, Charles could not help but think that the daemons and spirits he had, as a boy, tried in vain to conjure, had finally come to do his bidding. The thunder echoed the formulae of Cornelius Agrippa, Albertus Magnus, and Paracelsus; it echoed his own voice, as he spoke, and chanted, and finally shouted the spells, all to no avail.

And then, while trying to learn more about the father he had never known, Charles discovered the tattered remains of a sheaf of notes. Once he read them, he was possessed of an unquenchable desire to follow the trail the elder Frankenstein had blazed, and to find its end.

The creature was the result.

The door to the chamber crashed open. The odor of burning oil overcame the crystalline scent of lightning and rain. Carrying a tin lantern, Paulus limped into the room.

"The storm is coming," he said.

"Go raise the mast," Charles said. A blast of cold, wet wind chilled the room.

"Yes, milord," Paulus whispered.

The creature moved.

Charles started, but the immense being merely leaned forward, almost but not quite into the candlelight, impelled by desperation.

Charles gestured abruptly to the creature. "And take him out of here."

The creature rose obediently, his slowness the result of his great size and mass rather than of any hint of defiance. Zahlus took another draught of wine and pointedly ignored the figure looming above him; Charles found himself caught by the creature's penetrating, pleading gaze.

"Tonight . . ." The creature's voice was thick and rough, his words halting. His speech gave evidence that his mind was as pathetically reduced as his form was massively increased. Even Charles, who understood the potential of the creature's brain, had reluctantly come to believe that something had gone wrong, as so many other things had gone wrong with his creation.

He felt as responsible for the creature's pain as he was for its existence. And thus he was here, tonight, waiting for the storm and the lightning to reach their peak so he could complete this last experiment.

"Tonight," the creature said again.

"Yes," Charles said. "Tonight."

I cannot see out, for the single tiny hole—one could not dignify it by calling it a window—is above even my reach. Now and again—more and more frequently—lightning pushes away the clutching darkness, but only for a moment at a time. I long for sunlight and green trees, the singing of birds, the whisper of the breeze across a meadow. But perhaps my fate is darkness.

The dungeon is cold, even colder than the chamber whence I came, and though I can more easily withstand extremes of heat and cold and weather than the frail humans who put me here, the chill penetrates my ragged clothing and permeates my being, as if I were in terror. And perhaps I am. I have dreamed for so long of the moment that now approaches. I have dreamed . . . for all of my existence.

The thunderstorm crashed violently around the castle. Charles leaned out the window and looked into the sky. The wind lashed his face; the rain plastered his hair against his skull.

Charles climbed the stone stairs two at a time. He had climbed from the chamber to his laboratory so often that he no longer noticed the unevenness of the steps. Each tread was worn down half a handsbreadth in its center, and some collected puddles of condensation and rainwater. Charles was oblivious to all that now. Zahlus followed more slowly, though he was nearly as familiar with the irregularities of the path. He did not pause to pick his way carefully; rather, he moved slowly and deliberately, nonchalantly.

Charles tried, as he always tried, to ignore Zahlus's pose of disinterest. His nerves overcame his control.

"Hurry!" he cried.

The laboratory, fully three times the height of a normal room, took up the whole area of the tower's highest level. Heavy beams formed the roof, across which gusts of wind drove successive waves of rain.

The laboratory required no torch, no light. Suspended above, a great silver sphere glowed eerily. It drew power mysteriously from the air, from the earth, from the aether. Above it, the lower end of the mast projected through the room. When the two halves of the mast joined, they would carry to the globe the power of the storm.

Zahlus entered the laboratory, breathing heavily from his slow climb up the stairs.

"Really, Frankenstein, you must find yourself a laboratory in more civilized environs."

Charles looked at him, raising one eyebrow. "Indeed, Zahlus? No doubt you are right. Do you suppose the University of Geneva would welcome us? Or perhaps Berlin would support my work."

Zahlus stopped, taken aback, for Charles seldom defended himself against his witticisms. Zahlus had always taken that to mean Charles had no reply, when in truth the younger scientist had deliberately refrained from retaliation. At first he kept his silence out of respect for the other's age and accomplishments, later—when any respect he felt had been blasted away by Zahlus himself—out of his need for the older man's knowledge and skills.

After tonight I will no longer need him, Charles thought,

and then I will make myself rid of him. He cannot denounce me for my experiments without admitting of his own guilt. I will be safe once more, and free.

The wires leading from the mast glowed red-hot with electricity spilling from the aether. Charles turned his attention to the galvanometer. Its needle jumped, and then, as if impelled by the great roar of thunder overhead, spun over and quivered against the stopping-pin that marked the highest reading.

"Now!" Charles exclaimed.

Choosing to ignore Charles's unaccustomed show of backbone, Zahlus moved to the dissecting table, where a shrouded figure lay. Charles joined him. In an attitude resembling reverence, they drew aside the sheet.

Just above the table, a silken sling suspended a figure as different from the creature as one of Michaelangelo's sculptures compared to a piece of field-stone unearthed and scratched and broken by a plough.

The translucent linen concealed yet accentuated the new being's magnificent form. Charles beheld a cocoon, ready to free a butterfly such as the world had never seen.

Zahlus stared at the being.

"Now this, my dear Baron, this is a better piece of work altogether." Zahlus's tone arrogated to himself their mutual achievement, as if Charles were no more than a paid assistant. "I think you must admit, my boy, that I did better in obtaining its brain, the brain of an innocent, than you did scrabbling in charnel houses for the brain of your . . . whatever you choose to call it. And as for its body—"

Zahlus's eyes and his mind stripped the new being naked in a way that offended Charles as deeply as if the doctor had torn away the winding cloth with his hands.

Charles clenched his fists. "Will you be quiet!"

Zahlus looked across at him, blinking his bleary eyes, irritated by Charles's newfound aggressiveness.

"No," he said in a loud and penetrating whisper. "No, you're quite right. We mustn't disturb the child—on her wedding night."

Zahlus chuckled at his grotesque witticism. He grasped the handle of the winch and turned it, raising the new being high above the table so she hung, swaying slightly, just beneath the globe. His chuckle rose to laughter.

Charles forcibly controlled the furious trembling of his hands.

"Join the masts!" he cried to Paulus, on the battlements above.

A great crescendo of thunder, somehow seeming to begin before the flash of its accompanying lightning, shook the castle, the instruments, and Charles's soul. Yet he welcomed the sound, for it drowned out Zahlus's awful laugh.

Suddenly the mast glowed red, then yellow, then white-hot. The current, the power, poured unchecked from the aether into the globe, which concentrated it, intensified it, and poured it forth into the new being. Charles's creation, despite its tight restraints, jerked convulsively, ripping linen and silk. Another bolt hit the mast, and another, and the mast itself blasted apart, tearing a hole in the roof. Rain and wind screamed into the laboratory.

The new being could never survive this passage with anything of its body left intact! The tetanic contractions of its muscles would break its bones and rip apart its ligaments and tendons. Charles lunged forward. Zahlus apprehended his intent before he did himself, and thrust himself into Charles's path.

"Stay back, you fool!" the doctor cried. "You'll kill yourself!"

Charles struggled against Zahlus's powerful grip.

But he had pressed himself so unremittingly for so many months that he approached nervous exhaustion. Zahlus, despite his age and libertine ways, outmatched his strength. Charles struggled in his grasp as the new being, its wrappings torn to shreds, convulsed again and again.

"She'll die!" he cried. "If I don't save her, she'll die!"

"Let it die!" Zahlus shouted. "If it dies, you can make another! If you die—"

Suddenly a bolt of lightning crashed down directly into the globe, which churned with colored fire.

With his last iota of strength, Charles shoved Zahlus away. The doctor crashed to the floor, uttering an obscenity. Charles took a single step toward the table.

Awe and terror froze him.

The new being glowed. Her form relaxed to stillness, though the electricity still coursed through her from the sky. At first a soft warm light glimmered between the broken bandages, so faint it might be taken for hallucination or wishful fancy. But the light increased until it poured from the being like a phosphorescent liquid, until Charles believed it could become no brighter. And still its intensity increased. The bandages became as glass, and the new being radiated a cold, white incandescence.

I leap, and leap again, until finally my fingers clutch the bars of the dungeon's tiny window. I drag myself awkwardly upward, till I can see the sky. Rain blows through the open bars, touches my skin, and trickles down my face. It tastes of the clean open air, of forests and mountains.

Suddenly an immense bolt of lightning forks and twists toward the earth. A tingling touches my fingers, as if the essence of the lightning were spreading over the stone, thence to me.

The tingling is rather pleasant. I have few enough memories of pleasant sensations, that I give myself to this one, pressing my body to the cold stone and my forehead to the iron bars.

But suddenly the pleasure turns to pain. My hands clench and I am trapped. A searing heat turns to agony that increases without limit until it transcends my heightened perceptions. My clumsy body jerks and thrashes against the wall. I am burning—

Just as suddenly the pain ceases, and I am transported by the quintessence of peace and life. My hands relax; I slide to the floor. I lie still, my strength gone, my substance perfused by a shadowy coolness.

The glow emitted by the new being was as brilliant as the sun reflecting from glacial ice. Slowly it faded. Charles stood paralyzed. He feared the lightning's power had resulted in destruction and death, rather than life.

Behind him, Zahlus clambered to his feet and stumbled toward the table, toward the being, toward *her*. His actions roused Charles from his awe. He sprang forward and shouldered Zahlus out of his way so he himself would be the first to touch her. Even if she were dead, he could not bear that Zahlus touch her before he did. He grabbed an axe and severed the line to the winch. As the new being drifted to the ground, the brake thumped, slowed, and stilled like a dying heartbeat. The new being lay limp and lifeless.

Charles pulled the bandage gently aside. The first unwinding of the cloth revealed her eyes. They lay closed and still, the long dark lashes brushing her cheeks. Charles caught his breath at her beauty.

"Yes . . ." Zahlus whispered. "Altogether, a better piece of work." He reached out, one finger extended, as if to prod her. "Does it live?"

Charles grabbed Zahlus's wrist with a power he hardly knew he had.

"Wait," he said. "Look."

Beneath the unraveling bandages, her hand twitched.

Zahlus made an ugly sound of disappointment disguised by sarcasm. "Reflex. A momentary galvanic reaction. She has no more life than the detached muscle of a dead frog."

The new being opened her eyes.

The pupils had dilated completely. As Charles looked into the new being's empty eyes, he feared Zahlus was right. But the pupils gradually contracted. The violet irises appeared to radiate the energy of the storm. Charles blinked—and when he looked again, the eerie light had spent itself. And her eyes! One was green, the other azure.

The eyes focused abruptly, staring straight at Charles. This was no galvanic response.

His experiment had succeeded.

In exaltation, Charles cried, "On a night like this, men can become gods!"

The new being struggled violently against the straps and bandages, then fell back exhausted. Equally drained, trembling with the reaction to what he had done, Charles permitted Zahlus to help release her from the sling.

A short while longer, Charles reminded himself. Only a short while longer.

The soothing coolness dissipates and I feel once more the cold stone beneath me. My body aches, for granite will bruise even my stolid flesh. The storm is passing. The lightning is fainter, and the thunder peals long after each diminishing flicker of illumination. I push myself painfully to my feet. If the Baron kept his promise, his work is done. He has created another creature like me, someone to share the life of an exile from human society. Now I must keep my promise, to leave forever and take her with me, to a place where we never again will affront the delicate sensibilities of human beings.

I will give her the help I so desperately needed when Charles Frankenstein brought me to life. She will have much to learn. She will be afraid, as I was. But we are kin, and surely she will not fear me.

I rise, I stand, my knees trembling with unaccustomed weakness. I wish only to fall again, to sleep, until my body heals itself. But my promise impels me. My promise, and . . . something else. I am drawn from this wretched dungeon, upward, into the chamber in which I suffered so much pain. I would never enter it again, if I could help it.

I stumble on the stairs, for though I am stronger than any human being, I am less limber, and I have less practice at movement. And I am weary, so weary. The stairs pass beneath me. But the doorway is just ahead. From it escapes the blue ghost-light of the globe, the first sight I ever beheld. It stands in my mind as a symbol of torture. I endured so much from Frankenstein, beneath the unnatural light that bathes me once more.

Charles removed the rest of the bandages from the new being. Zahlus aided him, and it seemed to Charles that the doctor's hands lingered on her body longer than they need. Yet Charles could not bring himself to speak out in objection. If he accused Zahlus of lustful thoughts, Zahlus would deny it, call Charles a suspicious fool, and claim that Charles had similar designs. Of course that was ridiculous. The new being was no more than an experiment, his creation, an advancement of science in which he, personally, must show a complete and utter disinterest.

But . . . her form was perfect, her face enchanting, her skin the smoothness of deep-flowing water.

Her hair stood out around her head, still charged with static electricity. Charles reached out to smooth it. Sparks sprang to his hand, both shocking and startling him. He drew back, reflecting, There will be plenty of time to smooth and brush it later. He imagined brushing it himself, imagined her leaning back against him, the warmth of her body soaking into him.

Charles felt himself blushing violently. He tried to keep his back turned to Zahlus, for Zahlus had many times ridiculed Charles's transparent emotions. The fairness of his skin revealed every change in his humours. He had no control over his complexion, and he was in no mood to be ridiculed tonight. It was preposterous for him to feel any emotion whatever for the new being. He had seen her naked at every stage of her creation. He had seen beneath her skin. Besides, he was a doctor. He had dissected female corpses. The human body held no mysteries for him.

Yet in simple fact, the new being was the first and only living woman he had ever seen revealed. He could hardly take his gaze from her. She seemed mysterious in a way he had never imagined. And to touch her was like holding a bolt of lightning in his hand.

"Zahlus! What are you doing?"

Zahlus moved his hand before the new being's face, one finger extended upward as if he were practicing mesmerism upon her.

"Testing her reflexes, my dear boy. Watch her eyes."

He moved his finger to the right. The new being's eyes remained fixed, staring straight ahead, then suddenly the focus shifted and her gaze darted to the right. Zahlus moved to the left. Her eyes lost their focus, and she stared deep into the far corner of the room. Then the direction of her attention again shifted abruptly toward Zahlus's upraised finger.

"I fear she has some neural impediment. The motion of her eyes is most unnatural—very mechanical."

Before Charles could respond, Zahlus was staring toward the doorway of the laboratory. Zahlus stepped past him, taking the hand of the new being and raising it as if he were presenting her to the highest monarch of the continent.

Zahlus spoke. "I give you the bride of darkness! I give you —the new Eve!"

Charles spun around.

The creature stood in the doorway, half concealed by shadows. Charles nearly swooned.

Where is your scientific objectivity, Frankenstein? he thought. This is what you built her for. This—not mere animation—is the culmination of your experiment!

The creature shuffled into the ghostly light of the globe. While the new being seemed to radiate light, the creature absorbed light and brought upon himself a hideous, unearthly pallor.

The creature stared at the new being, as entranced as Charles and Zahlus.

"My—my friend . . ."

Charles shuddered at the rough voice of the creature, yet he forced himself to speak.

"Yes," he said. His voice shook. "Friend."

The creature lumbered closer to the new being.

For a moment she did not move. Her eyes appeared unfocused; she gazed fixedly into the corner where Zahlus last had drawn her attention.

The creature stopped.

The new being's gaze flicked from the empty corner and settled upon the creature. Her eyes focused. She took an abrupt, mechanical step away from the creature, who followed her anxiously.

"Don't be so impetuous," Zahlus said, chuckling.

The creature reached for the new being. His clumsy hand closed around her wrist. Charles gasped, fearing he would rip her arm from its socket.

The new being screamed and flung herself backward, twisting out of the creature's grasp.

Charles leaped between them.

"Get back, you imbecile!" he cried. He knew he could never turn her over to the creature for whom he had constructed her.

The creature seemed not to hear him. He tried to move around Charles, to reach the new being. His lips formed the single word *friend*, but he uttered no sound.

Charles struck him across the face.

The creature stopped. He gazed upon the new being, who stood stiff with terror, looking wildly for escape. The pleading expression on the creature's face changed gradually to comprehension, and finally to rage.

"No! Not . . . not my friend! Hate me!" He advanced on Charles. "You lie!"

He shouted an inarticulate protest of rage and pain. The sound echoed in the laboratory, louder and more penetrating than every rumble of the night's thunder. The creature turned around, as if searching for the source of his agony. He fixed his gaze upon the globe. Zahlus grabbed his arm, but the creature shook him off like a piece of soggy garbage.

The creature's fury erupted into violence. He grabbed the bench, lifted the heavy carven wood above his head, and flung it across the room. It crashed into the framework that suspended the globe. The supporting arm began to swing.

"The globe!" Zahlus cried in horror.

The globe rocked slowly, like an animate creature uncertain of its path. Zahlus took one step toward it, then, as it made its decision and toppled from its base, the doctor pitched himself backward, trying to escape.

The globe smashed against the wall. A fireball erupted, crashing through the roof. Charles swept the new being against his body, flinging them both down so they escaped the destruction. The globe exploded, louder than any thunder, and shards of shattered metal hurtled over his head.

Then all fell silent, but for the insane ringing in Charles's ears. The fumes of his chemicals mixed and spread, stinging his eyes.

He turned, and the heat of the burning room hit him full in the face. The more volatile chemicals ignited, heating all the others past their flash points. A container of kalium burst into flame, shattering a jar of natrium. The protective layer of oil flowed away and the metal exploded on contact with the air. Multicolored sparks scattered across the floor. Charles's equipment collapsed into a conflagration of such heat that even iron and steel softened, melted, flowed, and finally burned.

"Zahlus!" Charles shouted. "Zahlus, we must escape!" He dragged the new being to her feet. She stared into the fire, confused and fascinated by the colors and the movement.

The explosion had broached the wall of the tower, rending the stone wall like delicate fabric. The wind blew gusts of rain into the fire; the rain erupted in clouds of steam. As the broken beams of the ceiling sagged, a twisting figure fell and vanished, screaming, into the smoking wreckage. Charles took a step toward the barrier of fire, as if to rescue Paulus, then cursed himself as a madman. No one could penetrate those poisoned gases and survive.

"Zahlus!" he shouted again, peering into flames of scarlet and yellow and blue, white-hot steam, thick black smoke.

Beneath a great block of fallen granite, Dr. Zahlus moved. His hand scrabbled weakly at a corner of the stone, seeking to push it from his crushed body. Blood flowed from his nose and mouth. The fabric of his coat began to char.

Zahlus moved his hand as if to brush the heat away, or to extinguish it like a match. Red fire clambered up his arm. Zahlus writhed beneath the block, trying desperately to escape the heat and pain. He looked directly at Charles. He reached out with his burning arm.

Another beam fell into the fire between them. Charles could not reach Zahlus, any more than he could rescue Paulus. He drew away.

For an instant the new being resisted, mesmerized by the destruction. Abruptly, she fainted. Charles dragged her from the burning laboratory, into the dark passage, down the steep stairs.

Somehow he managed to get her to the foot of the tower and outside into the courtyard. High above, the fire still raged.

Charles's groom, Jan, groggy with sleep, half dressed in breeches and nightshirt, stopped before him. He mouthed words that Charles could not hear.

Whatever he was saying, it seemed terribly unimportant now. Though Charles had not seen the creature perish, he could no more have survived than Zahlus. Only Charles and the new being had escaped.

I'm free, Charles thought. Free of Zahlus, free of the creature! Finally, completely, free!

"Let it burn," he said to Jan.

He fell into a deathly swoon.

Chapter 2

Charles Frankenstein awoke as if from a dream. Cool linen lay smooth against his cheek and his palm; a thick feather-bed warmed him. The embers of a dying fire snapped comfortably in the hearth. He lay in his bed with his eyes closed, as he always did for the last few moments before he rose, marveling over the luxury in which he found himself. It was all quite different from what he had endured as a youth.

If only the ringing in his ears would cease, everything would be perfect. He must have indulged a touch too heavily the night before. And the fire, poorly built, sent smoke drifting into his bedchamber. He frowned. A headache, a smoky fire, and nightmares served to mar his satisfaction. Irritated, he flung himself over and sat up.

Last night had been all too real. Acrid smoke still clung to him, and his naked body was bruised and abraded. The pale gray light of a cloudy autumn afternoon seeped between the windowshades. Charles threw aside the bed-clothes, jumped to his feet, and nearly fell. He staggered from weakness.

The door opened.

"Milord, are you all— Oh!"

Mrs. Baumann turned away, covering her eyes. Holding the bedpost to steady himself, Charles snatched up his dressing gown, flung it around his shoulders, and held it closed.

"I am decent, Mrs. Baumann. Perhaps in future you should knock."

"I was worried—you were overcome by the smoke. You slept so deeply—and then I heard a shout—"

His housekeeper faced him again. Her cheeks were scarlet with embarrassment. Charles, too, felt embarrassed, but feigned indifference.

"You needn't concern yourself." He struggled to keep his voice completely even. "What of the young lady?"

Mrs. Baumann stiffened. Charles saw an outburst of indignation coming on, and he spoke quickly to deflect it.

"She is my *patient*, Mrs. Baumann. Where is she?"

"In the blue room, milord. She still slept, last I looked."

The blue room was down the hallway, around a corner, and up a flight of stairs. Mrs. Baumann had put the new being as far from Charles's rooms as she possibly could without exiling her to a disused part of the castle.

"Prepare the red room. When the young lady wakes, she will move there."

Mrs. Baumann prepared to object, for the red room lay immediately adjacent to Charles's.

"Mrs. Baumann!" Charles said sharply. "She has been through a dreadful ordeal! She cannot be off alone in the hinterlands of the castle. With time and care she may recover."

"Very well, milord," Mrs. Baumann said, her disapproval plain. She left the room.

The new being slept soundly and silently in the blue bedroom. Charles sat nearby, watching her by the light of a candle. The static energy had dissipated from her dark hair, which now fanned smoothly across the pillow. Yet when Charles reached to push an errant lock from her forehead, he felt as if a powerful charge passed from her skin to his. In the dim light, she fairly glowed.

Her breathing was regular, her heartbeat strong and

smooth. But he did not yet know if her mind had survived her reanimation. He was tempted to try to wake her. But she possessed elements of the wild animal about her, and, like a wild animal, she slept to heal herself.

He sat down to watch her, but memories of the night continued to pass across his sight. Zahlus, reaching toward him, his hand grasping, clutching for life, burning—

Charles shivered. He shook his head to drive off the visions. Zahlus had tormented him at every opportunity, and while Charles would not have sentenced the foulest murderer to death by fire, neither would he pretend to himself that he was anything but glad to be rid of the older doctor.

Free, Charles thought again. Free.

He would give Zahlus a decent burial, if anything of him remained to be buried. Even Paulus would have a grave, if the minister did not refuse to bury him in consecrated soil. The villagers held to cruel and stupid superstitions; to them, Paulus was the spawn of the devil, his crippled body a reflection of a twisted, evil soul. No doubt the minister would object to interring him in the churchyard . . . but the objections might be overcome by a judicious contribution to the poor box. Charles shrugged. Trivial matters, to be dealt with later.

As for the creature: If anything remained of his bones, Charles would kick them apart and leave them for the rats to gnaw.

Lightning flickered, and thunder rumbled in the distance as the storm moved slowly away. Charles glanced out the window, willing the weather to clear.

When he lowered his gaze from the sky, the new being had opened her eyes. She stared straight ahead, terrified by the sound of thunder.

Catching his breath, Charles leaned toward her. The motion attracted her attention, and she stared full into his eyes.

Her expression softened, changing from fear to wonder. No one had ever looked at Charles as the new being looked at him. His heart pounded desperately.

The firelight glowed upon her exquisite beauty, her darkly exotic complexion. The mechanical flicking of her eyes had ceased. Charles fancied he detected intelligence behind her eyes.

She moved her hand, tangling it in the sheet. She moved it this way and that, trying with increasing frustration to free herself. Charles touched her arm to soothe her, then drew back the bedclothes. She reacted like a child to whom a surprise has been revealed. She raised her hand and held it before her face, moving and turning it. She smelled it. She put her tongue to the palm, then drew back startled when she felt the touch. She seemed to realize that the hand was a part of her. Charles revealed her other hand. She touched the fingertips together. Suddenly she laughed.

Yes, Charles thought. Like a child. Exactly like a child. But an intelligent child, a child who can be taught, who can be brought up without superstitions and prejudices and restraints.

She reached out to him. Charles sat very still as she touched his forehead, his temple, his ear. She stroked the pale hair of his eyebrow. She touched his cheek. Her fingertips brushed his fine blond stubble. She put her hand to her own cheek. Charles could imagine the silken smoothness of it.

Lightning flickered in the distance and a gradual roll of thunder answered. The new being started, glancing toward the window as if prepared for an attack. Her eyes, though exquisitely human, retained somehow the wildness of an animal. Charles saw that the thunder brought back memories to her, too.

"Do you understand me?" he said softly. "I don't know if you can understand. . . ."

She looked at him and her lips parted. She spoke—she spoke! Never mind that her voice was a hoarse unpracticed whisper; never mind that her articulation was awkward.

"Understand," she said.

Charles held back a shout of joy and triumph. She spoke, and she understood! She possessed language, the ability that separated human from beast.

"You've had a dream," he said, seeking to drive out with his intensity her frightening memories of her first few minutes of life. "A terrible dream. But now you're safe."

"Safe," she said.

Did he imagine it, or had her voice turned faintly quizzical, as if she questioned his assurances?

"Safe," he said again. "You must rest. You must sleep."

"Sleep," she repeated, her eyes already closing.

Dark and mysterious against the snow-white pillows, she fell asleep. Charles watched her. He felt as if he could quite happily sit watching her forever and never ask another thing from life.

The maids, having taken away the smoke-stained drape in which Charles and Dr. Zahlus had wrapped her, had dressed her in one of Charles's white silk nightshirts. Mrs. Baumann had decreed that clothing her in a man's garment was less improper, if only slightly, than putting her to bed in nothing at all. Fatigue, nervous exhaustion, and the necessity of keeping watch over his patient had excused Charles, for the moment, from explaining how he came to be caring for an unaccompanied young woman who arrived in the dead of night in a storm, bringing with her neither luggage nor a lady's maid.

He set himself to fabricating a tale.

It was not only the servants who would wonder about his

visitor. When he introduced her into society, she must have a background.

He took in her every detail. Her hands lay outside the bedclothes, half covered by the long ruffled sleeves of his nightshirt. Broken, torn fingernails marred her long and fine-boned hands, but time and care would remedy that defect. The ruffles covered the bandages that remained around her wrists. He suspected that the scars beneath would not be very prominent; he hoped they would barely show.

Charles watched over his creation, wondering how he and Zahlus could have been so blind. Even before her animation, they should have realized she was destined for greater things than they originally planned.

He drew the bedclothes over her hands and around her shoulders, then settled back to watch her till dawn.

"To think of throwing her at that . . . daemon," he said softly. "I must have been mad."

I feel the heat of fading fire, and the chill of autumn rain. Around me it is dark. A nearby ember is my only evidence that my sight remains. A drop of rain falls upon it; droplet and ember vanish together in a hiss of steam.

The beams and stones that destroyed Zahlus and nearly crushed me also saved me from the blaze. After I destroyed the cursed globe, the ceiling collapsed and formed a barrier against the flames. And still the heat was terrible. Smoke overcame me; I feared I would die. Here I have lain—how long?

I press upward until the ashy litter atop me slides away. The heavy smell of smoke surrounds me—smoke, burned chemicals, wet earth and stone, and the penetrating odor of burned flesh. Zahlus is gone, dead, burned. For that I rejoice. But Frankenstein escaped. I saw him, safely beyond the flames, before I fell. He is neither courageous enough nor foolish enough to have tried to rescue Zahlus from his doom.

But perhaps I must rejoice that Frankenstein still lives. He saved the being who was meant to be my friend. And though she saw me and feared and loathed me instantly, how can I blame her? I had hoped she would be different from all the humans who despise me, I hoped she would be more than human. If she were, Frankenstein would have had to make her so. Of this he was incapable. Or unwilling. If any blame is to be laid, it must be laid to Charles Frankenstein.

I cannot wish her dead. She is the most beautiful thing I have ever seen in my life. She must never know I love her. She would find the idea repellent. So I will flee again. Perhaps I will go to South America, as I promised Frankenstein, not because I promised (he did not keep his promise, so I cannot be held to mine), but because my reasons for going there are no less valid than they were when I conceived the notion. There is said to be a race of giants living in the mountains there, among whom I hope to be accepted as I can never be accepted here. It is true that I had hoped to go with a new friend, but if I must go alone . . . then that is my lot in life.

The darkness eases; dawn is coming. I must leave Frankenstein's tower before anyone comes to see what the fire has spared.

Sunlight glimmered around the edges of the heavy curtains, but Charles neither secured them to keep in the darkness nor opened them to let in the light. He heard, but took no notice of, the clatter of a horse's hooves on the cobbled courtyard. The new being mesmerized him with her presence. His mind raced like a runaway horse through the possibilities implied by her existence.

The door to her chamber flew open.

"The news of your fire drove me from my bed before I'd fairly slept, old man—God in heaven, Charles, you look dreadful!"

William Clerval, Charles's oldest friend, with whom he had roomed at university, stared at him in shock.

William made a policy of never being shocked by anything.

"I'm perfectly all right, Clerval."

Charles rose. But his knees buckled, and only William's stepping forward to support him kept him from sprawling flat on the floor.

"Yes, indeed, so I can see."

Charles recovered himself, but he did feel weak. He could not recall the last time he had eaten.

"Your groom told me you were injured."

Charles managed to chuckle. "Jan believes that if he shows sufficient solicitude for my health, I will promote him from groom to valet."

"And so you should—have a valet, I mean, though it should be someone less rough-mannered than he."

"I don't need a manservant!" Charles said angrily. "I can shave and dress myself."

"Indeed?" Clerval said. "The evidence for your claim is not immediately obvious."

"I'm tired of this argument, Clerval! We've had it too often before. No doubt your house could burn down in the middle of a rainstorm and you would emerge in spotless white satin with your nails freshly polished."

"No doubt I would," Clerval said with casual wave of one hand. "But, of course . . . I have a valet."

Charles started to retort, then perceived the absurdity of the entire conversation and burst into laughter along with his friend. "William," he said, "I can barely hold my own against my housekeeper. Spare me a valet, and accept that you may never make a gentleman of me."

"Perhaps not. I seem to have made a good start of it, but I'll not get to finish if you kill yourself with overwork."

The candle by the new being's bedside flared and sputtered, brightening the room for a moment before it finally died. Clerval saw the visitor and arched one eyebrow.

"Or—can one hope that the dedicated Charles Frankenstein has discovered the benefits of an oversufficiency of play?" He leaned over her. His predatory gaze made Charles most uncomfortable.

"She's a patient, Clerval! Come away, before you wake her."

He permitted Clerval to help him to the breakfast room. Out of the presence of the new being, he again became aware of the aching of his body and of his deep exhaustion. He sat wearily at the table and called Mrs. Baumann to bring hot chocolate and bread.

"It was good of you to come, William. Last night—"

"News of the fire is all over the city, but the details are . . . confused. What happened?"

"An accident. I was working with . . . dangerous chemicals. They reacted in a way that could not have been predicted. They exploded. . . ."

"Was anyone hurt?"

Charles nodded. "My father's old retainer—the crippled man who lived in the tower. He was killed in the explosion." He hesitated, letting the sweet steam from his chocolate rise around his face. "And . . . Zahlus."

"Good god! Zahlus, dead?"

"Yes. He was . . . crushed beneath the wall, when it collapsed."

Clerval laughed, to conceal his true reaction. "Why, I

always thought the old philanderer would die in bed—someone else's bed."

"I am sure," Charles said, "he would have preferred such an end."

They sat together in silence. Charles pretended to eat. William tore apart a loaf of bread to conceal his distress. His well-kept hands picked soft crumbs from the inside of the crust, as if he were doing a gross dissection of some new creature.

Charles pushed his chair back so hard that it toppled over and crashed to the floor. William looked up, startled. Without a word of explanation, Charles strode from the breakfast room.

He climbed the puddled stairs to his laboratory. The tower lay open to the sky, and sunlight beat down as hard as the rain of the previous night. The pungent odor of smoke permeated the air. Charles's carefully crafted instruments lay twisted and askew like the work of some demented sculptor. The sun raised steam from pools of rainwater soaking into the floor.

He had begun to hunt through the ruins before William caught up to him. William paused in the doorway and let his gaze fall on each remnant of gutted equipment.

"My dear Frankenstein," he said. "How very mysterious."

"My dear Clerval," Charles said, "you would consider a simple microscope mysterious."

Charles reached the bookcase, which by pure fortune had been against the wall farthest from the center of the explosion. The upper shelves had been shattered by falling debris; the lower ones were filled with singed, soaked books. His rarest reference works lay scattered and ruined on the floor.

He opened the cabinet that contained the most important volumes. Moisture rippled the pages, but the fire had spared his journals. He picked them up and held them in the crook of his arm.

"I only want these," Charles said.

William had not moved from the doorway. It was just as well. The fire had left gaping holes in the floor, and even where the planks remained they were weakened and treacherous. A whole section of the wall had collapsed; there, nothing had survived. There, Zahlus had perished. If the doctor's body could be found at all it was no doubt unrecognizable. Charles hoped the same was true of whatever remained of the creature, but he did not want to take the chance of William's encountering such a sight. He could explain away the equipment, for in truth William Clerval had little knowledge of and less interest in natural philosophy. But explaining away the bones of a giant would be a more difficult task altogether.

Charles joined Clerval by the stairs.

"And now . . . I intend to seal this place up, as a monument to pernicious follies."

"What in God's name were you doing in here?"

"Nothing 'in God's name,' I assure you." He descended; William followed. He knew he must offer some explanation. "I was pursuing secrets of the natural world. But the universe guards its secrets jealously, my friend."

"Like a woman," William said.

Beneath William's light and mocking jest, Charles could hear a more serious and questioning tone. He had had no time for his oldest friend for nearly a year; and now William put him on notice that he required an explanation of more than Charles's ruined equipment.

But Charles could not tell William, or indeed anyone else in the world, what he had done.

At the foot of the stairs, Charles sank down and buried his face in his hands. The damp weight of his journals slid away against the stone, like fallen cards. An inutterable weariness possessed him.

"Charles . . ." Clerval said gently.

"Nothing 'in God's name,' William," Charles said, in answer to the unspoken question.

"Come along." William raised him to his feet. But when he reached for Charles's journals, Charles snatched them back. He was desperately grateful for William's presence, and just as desperately terrified that William would read a few words of his notes, understand immediately what Charles had done, and hate and despise him for it. If William ever discovered what Charles's ambition had led him to, he would damn him.

He raised his head abruptly and peered intently at William, who stepped back reflexively, as if he did not recognize the being who stared at him with such tortured eyes.

"Come along," Clerval said again, recovering himself. "You need rest, Charles. A few hours' sleep and you'll be yourself again."

Halfway back to the house, he added, with his usual nonchalant humor, "A bath and a shave wouldn't hurt, either."

Clerval was quite correct: after resting, bathing, and shaving, Charles felt much better.

Charles entered the library, where William had already helped himself to the sherry. He sat in Charles's leather wing chair, reading a morocco-bound book. The blood rushed from Charles's cheeks: he feared that Clerval had somehow extracted his journals from their hiding place.

"Clerval!"

William glanced up, startled, but smiled when he saw Charles. He rose. He held a volume by Byron: *Manfred*, a recent addition to Charles's library.

Charles laughed at his own fears, reminding himself: William would no more understand my notes now than he would have this morning, when I as much as snatched them from his hands. Perhaps four people yet alive would understand them, and William is not one of the four. Before he ever realized what he was reading, he would be bored by it.

"Ah, Charles, there you are." He gestured with the book. "Have you read this? It's—magnificent."

"No. I've not had the chance. I've had very little time for reading, recently."

"Or for much of anything else, such as your friends." He put the book aside and regarded Charles critically. "But I must say, you look your old self again."

"Thank you, Clerval."

"Yes—entirely your old self. Complete with crooked neck-cloth."

He straightened Charles's neck-cloth.

"You're as solicitous as an old hen."

"And you should be grateful for it. When I took on the task of making you a gentleman, I hardly knew what I was faced with."

"Erasing the stain of bastardy is no easy job," Charles said. He tried to speak lightly, but the bitterness would never completely fade.

"I suppose I'll never convince you that the hint of illegitimacy merely serves to make you more romantic. You have no idea how disappointed I was when your parents were proved to be married after all. Charles, a dark trace of mystery fascinates people—particularly women."

"What shameless flattery, Clerval."

"Shameless flattery is effective, too." He shook his head. "No, that part was easy. But I never thought I would have to teach a man how to tie his own neck-cloth."

"I can hardly express my gratitude at your perseverance in the face of such formidable labors."

Clerval sighed. "I do persevere."

As they both burst into laughter, Mrs. Baumann entered the library.

"Dinner is served, milord."

"Thank you, Mrs. Baumann."

Still chuckling, the two young men left the library.

"My next effort," Clerval said, "must be to persuade you that you cannot go out in polite society with the stains of noxious chemicals on your hands."

Charles had worked with aqua fortis for so long that he barely noticed the yellow-brown blotches on his fingertips.

"The stains will wear away in a week or two," Charles said. "Then you can claim your effort successful. If I never see another retort of acid, I'll count myself a fortunate man."

Clerval glanced at him sidelong, frowning slightly. Throughout their entire acquaintance, Charles's overwhelming interest had been the study of natural philosophy. How strange he must find listening to Charles claim that he was no longer interested in his life's work.

They entered the dining room, an immense chamber that formed the heart of the oldest section of the castle. Candlelight reflected from the long oak table, like sunlight on silk; the wood gleamed with beeswax and generations of polishing. More often than not Charles dined all alone at the head of the long empty table. He was glad of Clerval's company tonight, but he thought the room would be altogether less lonely if he were dining with the new being.

He hardly spoke through dinner. At first, Clerval chatted of inconsequential things, but on receiving no reply he fell into silence till the end of the meal.

"You're right to wall up your tower," Clerval said suddenly.

Charles forced his attention back to the dining hall. "What did you say?"

"I said, you'll never discover the secrets of the universe in your tower. You won't get at them with chemicals and machines. Poetry and lust, women and wine—those are the ways to wisdom."

"Then you have undoubtedly achieved it."

Clerval laughed. "No," he said. "My experiments blow up in my face, like yours—but only my heart is wounded."

Charles had no chance to hear more about Clerval's failed experiments, for Mrs. Baumann came in to clear the table. Clerval blew her a delicate kiss. She ignored him disdainfully as she took her time collecting the plates.

"Was there something else, Mrs. Baumann?"

"Yes, milord. I took some supper upstairs for the young lady, sir . . ."

"And?"

"She still hasn't waked, milord. Hasn't waked all day."

"Thank you, Mrs. Baumann."

She left the dining room, her curiosity unsatisfied.

Clerval was not so easily put off.

"Do tell me about your guest, Charles."

"My *patient*, William. She is quite an interesting medical case. The physician at Brucor referred her to my care. She was found in the forest, wandering in a daze." He paused. William listened attentively to the fabrication, his reaction no more quizzical than usual. "She had apparently been struck by lightning. The experience robbed her of all memory. She knows nothing of herself—not even her name."

"Can you cure her?" Clerval asked.

"I wonder if curing is what she needs."

Clerval's lips quirked in a smile. "She *is* pretty . . . and if she cannot regain her memory, she might be taught a thing or two."

"She's remarkably beautiful!" Charles said angrily. "She might be taught everything, Clerval! Think of it! She might be made into . . . anything."

"The most pliant of mistresses."

"No! Can you think of nothing else? What do I want with a simpering housewife, or a courtesan? The first can be had for promises. As for the second—money will assure any degree of compliance. You yourself told me that. I saw enough of courtesans in Paris."

"You saw barely anything at all of them," Clerval said, smirking.

"And what I saw sickened me! To be eternally agreed with, deferred to—pandered to!"

Clerval raised one eyebrow. "Surely you do not wish ladies to argue with you?"

"There is no progress without challenge."

"Next time we go to Paris, I will find you a courtesan who will challenge you. You will have to pay extra for unnatural acts of such magnitude . . . but you can afford it."

"Unnatural acts! What is unnatural is that half the human species is brought up to believe itself inferior to the other half. But *she*—she has escaped those lessons. Her mind is no longer crippled. She might be taught what *we* know. She might dare to think what *we* think. I might make the new woman, Clerval. Free, independent, as proud and bold as a man—"

"My dear Charles, what a preposterous suggestion!"

"Imagine—a woman equal to ourselves. A fit companion—"

"For the genius of Frankenstein." Clerval burst into laughter.

Charles glared at him, then leapt from the table and stormed from the dining room.

Chapter 3

As still and quiet as a stalking beast, *she* watched the man sleeping in the chair nearby. He seemed familiar, though she did not precisely remember him. She knew him, just as she knew the meanings of the little silent sounds moving behind her eyes, each accompanied by an image. She touched her hand, thinking, *hand*. She touched the sleeve of the shirt, thinking, *nightshirt*. She remembered a moment when she did not understand that her hand was a part of her; and then another moment when she did not understand that the nightshirt was separate from her. But she did not remember precisely when those moments occurred, and she did not remember the moments clearly.

She was fascinated by the ideas, by the images, by the sounds in her mind. She tried to create noises that imitated them. She succeeded. The words she spoke resembled the words within her mind. She felt pleased with herself, and she felt pleased with her voice.

"Hand," she whispered. She touched her hair. "Hair. Finger." Gaining assurance, she spoke more loudly. "Skin." Delighted with herself, she bounced up and down on the bed. "Bed!" She reached out and touched the chair, hard enough to set it moving on its rockers. "Chair! Man!"

The man's eyes opened.

She gasped as the man awakened. He gazed at her.

"You *do* understand!" he said.

She wrapped herself in the bedclothes, angry at having her game interrupted.

"I feared," he said softly, "that you only imitated me. The first time you woke, you repeated only the last word I said to you. I was afraid you spoke without understanding. But you do understand me, don't you?"

"Understand," she said.

He reached out to her. She took his hand, stroking it with her fingertips, bringing it to her face to rub it against her cheek, smelling it, then touching the tip of her tongue to his palm. He tasted salty and warm.

His hand quivered abruptly, and he jerked it away.

"Why?" she said, not understanding his actions.

"Why what?"

"Why . . ." She made a quick back-and-forth motion with her hand.

"Why did I shiver?" His pale cheeks grew quite pink, and she did not understand that, either. "I . . . I don't know," he said. "You surprised me."

She touched his cheek again. His skin felt very warm. She expected the same scratchiness she had felt last time she touched him—when had that been? It was so difficult to remember—but his skin was nearly as smooth as hers. She touched her own cheek, then his.

The man smiled. "I shaved," he said. "I did not know if you would remember seeing me unshaven."

"Dream," she said. "I had . . . a dream."

"Yes. But it's over now, and I'm no dream. I'll help you, I'll teach you."

He started to talk to her. His words went on and on. She stopped listening. She hunched over and wrapped her arms around herself, for she felt hollow and unhappy.

His voice stopped, then began again. "What's wrong?"

"Hurt," she said. "Inside."

He bent over her, concerned. He felt her forehead and her wrist. She drew back, angry, wondering why he touched her face and hands when her inside hurt.

Suddenly he laughed.

"You're hungry! Is that it? It must be! Just wait, wait right there, and you will have your first meal."

He hurried from the room, calling, "Mrs. Baumann! Our visitor will dine!"

She watched curiously as light and activity transformed her dark, quiet room. The man went away, but several other humans—they were women; somehow she knew it, though she was not clear about why they were *women* and the man was a *man*—came in and bustled about, moved the pillows behind her, held out a mass of material into which they directed her to place her arms. She thought that she could do any of their actions as well as they could. She tried to push aside the bedclothes so she could rise and walk as they did.

"No, no, young miss," said one of the other humans, a very small and slender one with light brown hair pushed up under a stiff piece of material, the purpose of which was unclear. "You just stay right there and we'll serve you your supper in bed. Won't that be nice?"

She wondered if she were ever permitted to leave the confines of the bed. She longed to move, to explore, to test herself. She suspected she had great power in this body of hers. She wondered where the people went, when they vanished through the doorway. Where had the man gone? Where did the women go? The little brown-haired woman suddenly grasped a length of fabric attached to the wall and pulled it aside.

The new being gasped. Silver light poured through the wall. She would never have been able to imagine anything so beautiful and wondrous.

The little brown-haired woman raised a part of the wall. A gust of cool, invigorating air, permeated with entrancing scents and sounds, slipped into the room.

"Hannah! Close that window, you foolish snip! Exposing milord's guest to the night air!" The largest of the other humans, the one with the gray hair and the disapproving and suspicious demeanor, crossed the room, pushed Hannah aside, and slammed the window.

"No—no!" the new being cried.

"But, Mrs. Baumann," Hannah said timidly, "it's such a nice night, ma'am—maybe the last warm night of fall."

"Do as you're told! I'll have none of your back talk!"

Hannah's shoulders hunched and she looked at the floor. "Yes, ma'am."

The new being wondered what terrible power the gray-haired Mrs. Baumann had over other people. She was about to rise and open the window herself, to find out what would happen, when an even more entrancing scent distracted her attention. Another young woman carried a tray to her bedside.

"Sit up straight," Mrs. Baumann said. "How can we feed you if you don't sit still?"

The new being grabbed a handful of the nearest thing on the tray and shoved it into her mouth.

"God in heaven!" Mrs. Baumann cried. "It don't even know to eat porridge with a spoon!" She tried to take the tray away, but the new being jerked it from her hands. The food spilled from the cups and plates and splashed over the bedclothes.

Mrs. Baumann shrieked and rushed from the room, but the new being had almost ceased to listen to her or notice her.

The porridge tasted pleasantly warm. It eased the ache in her stomach, but it was not the source of the most wonder-

ful odor. A round red thing rolled across the bed. The new
being caught it as it fell off the edge. She bit into it. Sweet
tart juice spurted across her tongue. She crunched the flesh.
She finished it, core and all, in three bites. It was delicious,
though it was not what she had smelled either. She snatched
at a third piece of the food. It was more substantial than the
porridge, but part of it was too hard to eat. She had to rip it
with her teeth to free a mouthful. But it was the smell she
had been seeking. It tasted equally wonderful. She finished
it, gnawed the bone, and pawed through the spilled food
looking for more. When she found none, she looked at the
other serving maid, who huddled beside Hannah in the far
corner of the room. They shrank from her gaze. Then Mrs.
Baumann returned and they shrank from her, too.

"She ain't even civilized, milord!"

The man followed Mrs. Baumann into the room. The new
being felt happy to see him. She showed him the bone.

"Good," she said. "More."

"She never even waited for me to put the tray down, even
less to spread out her napkin!" Mrs. Baumann said. "She ate
an apple in three bites, core and all—Why, the seeds will
sprout right inside her!"

"Don't be absurd, Mrs. Baumann," the man said. He
came to the new being's side and smoothed her hair back
from her cheek, where porridge had struck a strand of it to
her skin.

"Is it meat you like best?"

"Meat?" she said. "Yes. More."

"She wants more, Mrs. Baumann," the man said. "Get
her what she wants."

"She'll make herself sick, milord, if she ha'n't done already!"

The man smiled. "I don't think so," he said. "We must be

patient with her. Give her what she wants, then help her bathe. I'll be in the library."

After the man went away again, Mrs. Baumann stood with her hands on her hips and glared disapprovingly at the new being. The two serving maids watched from the corner, then suddenly burst into giggles.

"Think this mess is funny, do you?" Mrs. Baumann said. "Well, 'tis you who'll have to clean it up! Go get tonight's leg of mutton off the spit and bring it here."

"But ma'am, it isn't done cooking!"

"I'll not repeat my order!" Mrs. Baumann said to Hannah. "If you speak out of turn again, I'll discharge you!"

The two young women scurried from the room. Mrs. Baumann stayed where she was, glaring angrily at the new being, who met her gaze without blinking and wondered why Mrs. Baumann was so angry.

Mrs. Baumann looked away first. "Like an animal, it is," she muttered. "Bedlam's where you belong, not in a baron's home!"

She watched the new being warily till Hannah returned.

At the sight and smell of the steaming leg of mutton, the new being forgot all the words and thoughts and questions. Her hunger overcame her. She seized the meat in both hands. She barely noticed how hot it was. She sank her teeth into it. The juice and fat ran down her chin, between her fingers, down her hands to her bandaged wrists, and over her forearms. It dripped onto the ruffled sleeves of her nightshirt and the fine soft fabric of her bed-jacket.

She tore at the meat and swallowed it, barely taking trouble to chew it. The fire had seared and crackled the outer meat, and the inner was blood-warm.

"Law!" Mrs. Baumann said. "Ain't it disgusting!"

The new being heard the threat in the voice. She looked

up, drawing her lips back from her teeth, and snarled a warning. Mrs. Baumann would not take the meat from her, as she had taken the fresh air.

"Don't spit at me, you little witch! I ain't afraid of spitting."

Keeping a wary eye on Mrs. Baumann, the new being bent over the meat again. As her hunger began to ease, she was once more able to pay attention to what was going on in the room around her. Hannah and the other serving maid carried in a large wooden tub, which they put on the floor before the hearth. Then they came back and forth from outside with buckets of steaming water, which they poured into the tub. She watched this process curiously as she gnawed the last, tenderest, rawest bits of meat from the bone.

"You've fair finished that, you beast," Mrs. Baumann said. "Milord's dinner, and ours as well."

The new being permitted Mrs. Baumann to take the bone —if she wanted the gristle that remained, she could have it, though there was little enough even of gristle. But Mrs. Baumann threw the bone aside and laid hold of her instead, pulling her from the bed. At first she complied, for she was anxious to leave it, and perfectly willing to shed the robe, upon which the grease had begun to congeal. She did not quite understand why the women had made her put it on, only to take it off her again.

"Hannah! Marie! Get yourselves over here! Hold her arms!"

Without warning, Mrs. Baumann grabbed her hair and one bandaged wrist and propelled her toward the wooden tub. The other two women, reluctant but obedient, took her arms and pulled her forward. She struggled against them, and shrieked, more in anger than in fear. They dragged her over the edge of the tub. She lost her balance and splashed down into the hot water.

Downstairs, Charles heard the angry cries and splashings and deduced that his guest would prefer some other activity to bathing. He paused with one foot on the bottom step of the long, curved staircase, then thought better of returning to the new being's room. The shrieks subsided; Mrs. Baumann no doubt had things well in hand, and she would not take well to his walking in on a lady's bath.

He returned to the library and sat before the hearth, staring into the black ashes. He had a formidable task ahead of him, he knew—perhaps even more formidable than that of creating the new woman. In creating her body, he had succeeded magnificently. But he must create her mind as well. He was impressed and intimidated by her strength and her animal magnetism. He feared he had brought into existence a creature so powerful that it could not be influenced by a mere man.

At a soft sound behind him he turned, expecting one of the maids or Mrs. Baumann.

He stared, transfixed, as *she* walked into the library, curious as a child, and as naked as a Grecian goddess. Her skin was a tawny gold. His impression of her as feline intensified, but she was not a lioness dozing in meager shade on a sunswept veldt. She was a tigress, gliding silently through the jungle.

She smiled when she saw him. She crossed the room. He could not help but stare at her, at the way the long muscles of her thighs lengthened and tightened as she walked; at the motion of her breasts. She sat on the hearth rug at his feet, completely unconscious of her nakedness, of her sex, of his own.

"Who are you?" she said softly.

Charles struggled to control himself, for his heart pounded and his breath came more rapidly than it should.

He felt a fool. He had *created* her! He had seen and touched more of her body than Clerval could imagine knowing of the most compliant of his courtesans. And yet the living being made him feel that he was in the presence of mysteries he could never hope to comprehend.

"My name . . . is Frankenstein," he said.

"Who am I?"

"I shall call you after the first woman," Charles said. "Eva. Your name is Eva."

She reached up, holding out her hand to him.

He remained motionless, afraid to touch her, afraid to take her hand.

For his own hands were trembling uncontrollably.

"Frankenstein," Eva said, testing each syllable carefully. "Frankenstein."

"Milord!" Mrs. Baumann's voice echoed in the hallway. "Baron Frankenstein, sir, she's got away!"

Eva's dark, arched eyebrows drew together into a frown.

The housekeeper hurried into the library. Bathwater soaked her apron. She looked most put out. When she saw Eva sitting naked at Charles's feet, her expression changed to outrage. "Look at the shameless thing! I no sooner went to fetch it a cloak—" She hurried forward, grabbed Eva's wrist, and jerked her to her feet. "Get up! Come and cover yourself, you filthy little creature!"

Eva twisted about, nearly freeing herself from Mrs. Baumann, but Charles roused himself from his fascination.

"No, Eva, you must do as Mrs. Baumann tells you. She is helping you."

Eva gazed into his eyes as if trying to comprehend what he was saying, but she stopped struggling against the housekeeper.

"Mrs. Baumann," Charles said, "you must be gentle with her. She doesn't understand about these things. We must teach her. You must help her learn to dress in polite society. Give her my gown from university. It will do till she's ready for fashion."

Mrs. Baumann put herself between Eva and Charles. "Take your eyes off her, milord! Look to the ground! I've heard of men blinded for less!"

Charles could not help but smile at Mrs. Baumann's superstitions. He did not avert his gaze.

Mrs. Baumann hurried Eva from the room.

Eva looked back once, pleading, but when Charles said nothing, she allowed Mrs. Baumann to lead her away.

I trudged all day through the forest, hiding by the side of the road whenever I heard the approaching sounds of humans or their beasts. Toward evening a horse came galloping so fast that it appeared around a curve in the path almost before I could conceal myself in the underbrush. It heard or scented me and plunged to a halt, snorting and rearing with rage and fear, nearly unseating its rider. It was a beautiful creature, small yet powerful, golden bay. Its ears lay flat back, then swiveled toward me. I felt sorry to have frightened it. Its rider, unaware of my presence, cried out in anger and surprise, regained his seat, pulled brutally on the reins till the horse's mouth frothed red, and lashed his mount's flank viciously till the horse screamed and sprang into a dead run, wild-eyed with pain and terror. Once more I have been the source of hurt to another living creature.

I saw no one else after that, a small boon of fate for which I was grateful. The sun set. I sought out a hollow between the roots of a huge old tree, pulled together dry leaves to form a bed, and lay down to rest. The leaves smelled of the summer sun. But as I slept the rain came. Now, in the first light of dawn, I am damp and cold and hungry. The leaves, which last night were so light and sweet-scented, have become a chill wet mass that smells of decay and death. Perhaps I should simply stay here and let myself dissolve back into the earth whence I came.

But I rise; where I am going I cannot tell.

The road stretches endlessly ahead, leading east. In the wilderness, where there are no people to be frightened by my form, I may find peace.

While I walk I gather acorns, crush them in my hands, and eat the bitter meat.

The sun rises higher, bringing to the forest a watery, diluted light. A few birds sing and call in the trees above. I wonder if I can make sounds such as theirs, if a whistle or a hum might serve me better and hurt me less than my rough and painful voice. Timidly, I try to copy their song.

The birds hear me and burst into flight, fleeing from me like every other creature.

The forest is silent, and cold.

Rinaldo was in real trouble this time. The boys surrounding him were too thickheaded to be distracted by his tricks. He had wasted his finest sleight-of-hand on them and they had not even noticed what he was doing. His wit was no match for their sticks, and an appeal to their good nature was useless when they believed they were doing the lord's work.

"Devil-spawn!" one of them cried.

"You're not a man, you're a daemon!"

From behind, a boy jabbed a stick between his feet and he fell sprawling in the road. Another boy laid his stick across Rinaldo's back, knocking the wind out of him. He struggled to his feet and raised his fists with feigned bravado. He much preferred to talk his way out of altercations, but this gang was in no mood to listen. They were well-grown boys of twelve or fourteen; the top of Rinaldo's head did not reach as high as the shoulder of the smallest.

"All right!" he said. "You want to fight, I'll fight! I'll take you on one at a time!"

The leader laughed and jabbed at him from the safe distance of the end of his staff. Rinaldo slapped the stick away. His resistance won him more blows.

"Want to fight fair, huh? Does your master the devil fight fair?"

If I knew a devil to call on, Rinaldo thought, I'd surely have him smash these brutes with lightning.

"I'll bet this one's got a tail and cloven hooves! Let's strip him and see!"

Rinaldo grabbed the nearest stick and shoved it back against its owner. The end rammed into the boy's chest and knocked him back, leaving Rinaldo in possession of the staff. He tried to use it to defend himself, to break through the circle and flee, though he knew he had little chance against so many foes.

The boys in front of him stopped stock-still. Suddenly they turned and fled, shrieking. Rinaldo watched, mystified. He looked at the stick. He could have fought off a single bully with it, or even a pair; but bullies gained strength from numbers. The stick would have had to spit sparks of blue light to frighten a whole gang. It was definitely a very ordinary stick of very ordinary wood.

And then Rinaldo heard a sound behind him. He turned.

The stick fell from his hands, and he stared in wonder at the man towering over him. In all his years of travel, all his years of living with fellow outcasts from society, he had never seen anyone like this. He was a giant, not only in height but in mass. He wore ragged, travel-stained clothes, and his face bore the scars of accident, fight, or treachery.

No wonder the gang had fled. Yet . . . Rinaldo saw no

hint of threat. The man gazed down at him, a troubled expression on his face. He glanced after the fleeing boys, then at Rinaldo again, as if to ask, Did they hurt you; as if to say, They have gone now, you are safe.

Rinaldo took a deep breath.

"Thanks for that," he said.

The giant cocked his head.

Why does he look so curious? Rinaldo wondered. Perhaps he doesn't understand the language—or perhaps he cannot understand at all. Or . . . perhaps he's just looking me over before he smashes me like a bug and walks on.

The giant's lips moved. He produced a rusty, incomprehensible sound. He tried again.

"Man . . . ?" he said slowly.

Rinaldo scowled and drew himself up to his full height. Saved from a gang of bullies to be insulted by a giant! he thought, irritated. Enough!

"Yes, I'm a man!" he said in a belligerent tone, and, when the giant merely continued to look at him with every evidence of friendly curiosity, he strode nearer and poked him in the knee with one finger.

"If you catch my drift!"

The giant silently frowned, more in perplexity than anger.

Rinaldo found the giant a most interesting fellow, and possibly useful to boot. Around here, anyone outside the limits of average was marked by evil, fair game for torment. The giant might also be considered a familiar of the devil, but even a zealot would think twice before trying to torment a giant. Even a dwarf might be safe with such a traveling companion.

"Now my name," Rinaldo said, "in case you're interested, is Rinaldo. What's yours, sir?"

The giant gathered strength to use his tortured voice. "No name," he whispered.

Rinaldo nodded sagely. "On the run, eh? Incog. Nothing unusual in that. You'll not find me pressing you for details. But I, myself, am traveling to Budapest. I intend to join a circus there. We can walk a bit together, if you like the company."

He started down the road. After a few paces, he glanced back. The giant stared as if mystified by having another human being speak to him in a civil tone.

"Come along," Rinaldo said, with a sweep of his hand and a courtly bow. "It's a long way to Budapest."

The giant followed, and they walked together down the road. Rinaldo had to hurry to keep up.

"Slow down a bit, fellow, your length of leg gives you the advantage of me."

The giant stopped instantly, sorrow and guilt plain on his face, and afterward slowed his pace considerably.

"You look like the circus type yourself," Rinaldo said, when he had regained his breath.

The giant shook his head slowly, not understanding.

"Strongman? Stake-driver? Stall-mucker?" Rinaldo saw that these terms meant little to the giant. A man with much to learn, he thought. And he's found the one to teach him. But I do wonder where he has been all his days, to get his growth and maintain such an innocence. "There's generally work for the likes of us, and no questions asked."

The giant listened silently to Rinaldo's explanations.

The road rose, and though the giant kept to his slowed pace, Rinaldo found it difficult to keep up.

"It occurs to me," he said carefully, "that since we are going in the same direction . . . a gigantic fellow like you could set a tiny little fellow like me right up on your shoulder and hardly know he was there. What do you think?"

Rinaldo reached up to the baffled giant.

"Give it a try, eh?"

The giant's great fingers closed around Rinaldo's hand with astonishing gentleness.

"Here we go!" Rinaldo said. "Right up there."

The giant swung Rinaldo up to his shoulder.

"Very comfortable, indeed," Rinaldo said, surveying the countryside from the unaccustomed height.

The giant stood still, not knowing what to do next.

"Carry on, then." Rinaldo patted the giant gently on the shoulder.

The giant suddenly understood what Rinaldo had in mind. A delighted smile spread over his weathered face, and he strode down the road. Rinaldo had once seen a picture of a sultan riding on the back of an enormous elephant; he had always wondered what it must feel like to be allied with such power. Now he knew.

They passed over the rise in the road and came upon the boys who had attacked Rinaldo. They argued and shook their sticks at each other, fighting over whether they had truly seen a giant, or whether the giant had been a vision brought on by the little daemon.

"Out of the way!" cried the little daemon atop the illusion. "Out of the way! We have business in Budapest!"

Metaphysical arguments abandoned, the boys took one look at Rinaldo and the giant and fled again, running even faster, if that was possible, than they had before.

Rinaldo burst out laughing with sheer joy.

"What a clever fellow," he said to the giant, fondly.

The giant responded to Rinaldo's friendship. He gathered himself to speak; he said, hesitantly, "Circus."

"Circus, indeed!" Rinaldo laughed again.

The giant began to make a strange, hoarse, ugly sound. Rinaldo felt afraid for a moment, but then he realized what the sound was, and he almost burst into tears of pity.

The giant was laughing, too.

Eva sat on the floor of her room, a large paper spread out before her. She touched each of its colored areas in turn, trying to make sense of them. Frankenstein had told her that this was the world. This she did not understand. The image the word brought in her mind was much greater and wilder. And it was not flat.

She raised her head. Frankenstein sat in a chair in the corner, watching her. She grew uncomfortable sometimes, in his penetrating gaze. He expected something of her that he would not explain.

"World?" she said. She touched the paper again. It crackled beneath her touch.

"Yes," he said smiling. "That is the world."

Eva jumped to her feet, ran to the window, and pulled aside the curtains. Beyond the cold glass the gray scene glistened. Eva thought it fascinating. Frankenstein still had not permitted her to experience it herself, though she had seen people out walking in it. She pointed.

"World!" she said emphatically.

Frankenstein frowned. Eva thought she had angered him by disagreeing, and this made her feel sad, but she pointed out the window again.

Frankenstein suddenly laughed. "Yes," he said. "I stand corrected. Come here, child."

He rose from his chair and knelt beside the paper.

"This paper is a map. A map is a representation of the world or a part of it. Do you understand?"

She squatted down beside him, intent and curious. He drew a quick sketch and showed it to her.

"Here is a map of your room." He touched the space between two lines. "This represents the door." He pointed to the door. "Here is your bed, here is the window, here is the hearth."

She glanced around the room, then at the paper.

"And this map is a map of the whole world. We are here, in a spot too small to see." He touched a place in the center of the map.

"Here?" Eva said, touching the map beside Frankenstein's finger.

Frankenstein nodded, obviously pleased.

"This line is a river, and this is a mountain. This spot is a city."

"River? City?" The words sparkled silently behind her eyes, bringing with them images of things she had never seen. Slowly she realized that he meant everything was shrunken down very small, and placed upon the paper. The lines represented images just as words did.

"I'll show you a river soon," Frankenstein was saying. "Even a city, eventually."

In abrupt comprehension, Eva smiled.

"You'd like that, would you," Frankenstein said. "All right, soon we'll go see a river."

But Eva barely heard him. Delighted and entranced by the idea of the map, she traced its lines with her fingers. If the spot in which she sat was so small that it could not even be seen, then the outside must be much larger than she had imagined—larger than she could imagine. It must truly be wondrous.

Untroubled by more gangs of stupid boys, Rinaldo and the giant passed into the countryside. For a while, Rinaldo felt as if every problem he had in the world had been banished when he met the giant. But as the day wore on, though the giant walked with a tireless stride, Rinaldo could not help but remember other difficulties. He could not distract himself with conversation, for his companion barely spoke. For several hours he talked on in a monologue, telling the giant about his travels, his stay with the Gypsies, his sojourn in Berlin, the circuses he had joined and left. But after a time even Rinaldo grew tired of his own voice. Besides, his talk kept drifting toward descriptions of food, and that only served to remind him of how hungry he was. His meager funds had run out two days before. He could subsist on very little for some time—he had certainly had enough practice—but his rations had been short for so long that his endurance, and his patience, were fast running out.

"I don't suppose you've got anything to eat with you, do you, my friend?" he said. "No, that's a foolish question, your hands are as empty as my wallet. Do you have even a few pennies?"

The giant dug in his pocket. Rinaldo's spirits rose. With a little money, they could reach Budapest in relative style. At the rate the giant walked, they were only a few days away.

The giant reached up and offered Rinaldo what he had taken from his pockets. The dry brown nuts clicked together in his palm.

"Acorns?" Rinaldo said, disappointed.

The giant nodded and made a careful gesture, urging Rinaldo to try the nuts. He even cracked two together and broke the meat free for his new friend.

Rinaldo, who would try almost anything once, gingerly put some of the acorn meat into his mouth. He had never tried to eat an acorn before—he had always thought they were poisonous. But if the giant had eaten them, so, no doubt, could he.

The bitterness spread across his tongue and nearly gagged him. He spat the acorn out, coughing and gasping.

"Is this what you've been living on, my dear comrade?"

The giant nodded.

Rinaldo's tongue felt shriveled. The worst thing about the acorns was that their taste lingered.

"There are limits," he said. "There really are limits. Comes a time when one must take one's fate into one's own hands." A rutted dirt path led off the road a short way ahead, and beyond a tangled line of trees sat a small thatched farmhouse. "Go over there," Rinaldo said. "Through the trees. You'd better let me down for a bit."

They passed through the trees to where they could see the cottage and the farmyard more clearly. It was a relatively prosperous place, the roof in good repair, the walls freshly whitewashed, a large kitchen garden behind the house, chickens freed from their coop to peck about in the yard. Exactly the sort of places he had stopped at, years before when he was much younger and more innocent, to ask for work in return for a meal. The good pious people always drove him off with brooms and sticks. After a few beatings, he still looked for the farm people, but he looked for them so he could avoid them.

At this farm, Rinaldo saw no one around.

"Stay here," he said to his companion. "If anything happens, run away. I'll meet you down the road."

The giant made no objection, though he also made no sign that he understood. Rinaldo moved cautiously from the concealment of the underbrush into the farmyard. He was more concerned about dogs than about the human inhabitants, but he reached the center of the yard without seeing any sign of life except the chickens. Fat ones, too, he thought, inspecting them without actually looking at them. Chickens, for all their stupidity, always knew when one was looking at them. He crept toward them. The chickens continued to peck at the ground, but their querulous clucks grew slightly louder, slightly more hysterical in a confused sort of way. He sidled closer. One of the chickens raised its head and looked to one side, to the other.

Rinaldo pounced. His hands closed on the nearest chicken. He snatched it up.

The door of the farmhouse crashed open.

"Stop, thief!" The goodwife snatched an axe from the woodpile and chased after Rinaldo.

He scampered back toward the bushes, the chicken squawking loudly, flapping its wings and pecking his arms and shedding feathers. Rinaldo plunged headlong across the yard, struggling to keep his hold on the terrified chicken.

"Stop, you wretched thieving little goblin!" She swung the axe. It whizzed past his head.

The bushes scraped his face as he barreled through them. The foliage crunched behind him as the goodwife followed.

The giant appeared from behind concealing bushes. The the crash of breaking branches ceased, the axe thudded to the ground, and the goodwife gave a terrible scream. Abandoning goblin, chicken, and axe alike, she ran for the house.

Rinaldo stopped, gasping for breath.

The giant gazed after Rinaldo's pursuer, who now fled in fear of pursuit herself. The giant's entire attitude was one of confusion and sadness at having frightened still another person.

The giant looked quizzically at Rinaldo, then at the chicken. He obviously did not know quite what Rinaldo had done. Rinaldo decided it would be better to explain too little than too much. The giant might be such an innocent as to misunderstand the difference between craven thievery and simple survival.

"But we do make a team, my friend, do we not?" He chuckled, delighted finally to begin to see his tormentors receive a taste of their own medicine.

Eva sat stiff and uncomfortable at a long, shiny table set with plates and silverware and lighted candles. Frankenstein stood nearby, watching her. She felt uneasy. She wanted to please him, but she did not know what he expected of her. She was dreadfully hungry, but instead of giving her something to eat, he had asked her what she wanted over and over again, until she satisfied him with her manner of asking and her pronunciation. Even then he would not give her food. He wanted her to behave in a particular way. She finally understood that he wanted her to put her hand on his arm and let him lead her, though she did not understand precisely why. She could walk perfectly well without his help. Then, after he led her into the dining room, she finally understood that he wanted her to sit in the chair he pulled away from the table. And now he simply watched her.

Mrs. Baumann entered the dining hall, carrying a platter from which drifted a scent so delicious that Eva's mouth watered and her determination to please Frankenstein vanished from her mind. She started up from the chair, reaching for the platter. Mrs. Baumann shrieked and leaped back, and Frankenstein put one hand on Eva's shoulder. She looked at him, stricken and confused.

"What will you do?" he asked.

She glowered. She had already told him what she wanted. Her stomach growled and her mouth watered; she longed to lunge for Mrs. Baumann and the delicious smell. She was so hungry she could barely think. All the sounds and symbols mixed together in her mind.

"I eat . . ." Frankenstein looked at her expectantly and she grabbed at the first word she could think of. ". . . chair!" As Frankenstein unhappily shook his head, Eva reached for the platter. Mrs. Baumann snatched it out of her reach. Frantically Eva sought another word. "I eat . . . curtains!" Again Frankenstein shook his head. Eva's hands trembled with her desire to wrench the platter from Mrs. Baumann's hands.

"I eat . . . chicken!" she said. A triumphant look spread across Frankenstein's face, and even Mrs. Baumann appeared, if not quite pleased, at least not so disapproving as usual. She put the platter down and picked up carving knife and fork. Eva reached over her plate and sank both hands into the meat.

"God in heaven!" Mrs. Baumann cried. She dropped the serving utensils with a great clatter, and slapped the table angrily with the flat of her hand. Startled, Eva sat back. She had made Frankenstein unhappy again.

"How do we eat?" he said.

This time she sat quite still as Mrs. Baumann carved the chicken and laid a small slice of meat on her plate. When Frankenstein nodded, Eva picked up her knife and fork as he had shown her. Her hands shaking, she cut the meat into absurdly small bites, speared one with her fork, and placed it into her mouth. This time Frankenstein not only nodded, but smiled.

Later, in a snug cave a safe distance from the road, Rinaldo basked in the warmth of the flames and enjoyed the sizzling scent of the roasting chicken.

"What a team we are." He laughed. "What a team."

The giant took his attention from the chicken long enough to gaze on Rinaldo fondly—but all of a sudden, the giant's eyes widened.

In the mouth of the cave, a lean wolf drew back its lips and snarled.

Rinaldo snatched a branch from the fire. Its glowing end burst into flame. The giant made a hoarse sound of terror and shielded his eyes from the fire.

"I can handle this," Rinaldo said.

He advanced upon the wolf, waving the brand in its face

until, still growling, it loped back into the darkness. Rinaldo flung the stick after it.

The giant watched in awe as Rinaldo swaggered back to the campfire and settled down to wait for the chicken to finish roasting.

The giant, too, hunched toward the heat, returning his gaze and his attention to the spitted chicken.

Rinaldo nearly dozed. Suddenly, the giant lunged forward, grabbed the spit, and buried his teeth in the chicken. Rinaldo watched, stunned, as the giant ripped off half the meat and messily gobbled it down. He made a noise that might have been, "Good," and then again might have been no more than a grunt of satisfaction.

I take the risks, you get the rewards? Rinaldo thought. Did I call us a team?

In a fury, he leaped up and swatted the giant on the nose, for all he might have been a huge dog.

"Not good!" he said. The giant scowled at him over the chicken, but it would have taken something much more fearful than the glare of an angry giant to stop Rinaldo. "We're a team! A team shares! What happened to sharing?"

The giant's scowl faded, to be replaced by his more customary look of vague confusion.

"Share?" he said, as if he had never heard the word.

"Yes, share! Didn't you think that I am hungry too?"

The giant looked at Rinaldo, at the chicken, and at Rinaldo again. Comprehension overcame him. Completely downcast, he thrust the mangled chicken into Rinaldo's hands.

"Eat food," he said.

Rinaldo took the spit, fastidiously detached one drumstick, and handed the rest back to the giant.

"I only want my share," he said. "Not all for me, not all for you. Share."

"Share," the giant said.

Rinaldo nodded. "Now, eat food."

The giant immediately plunged into the side of the chicken again.

Rinaldo gave a deep, pained sigh.

"Stop!" he said sharply.

The giant fairly scowled at him this time.

"Just because your clothes are dirty," Rinaldo said, "just because you are temporarily without means, does not give you reason to behave like an insufferable brute. We aren't savages, whatever others may call us. We are civilized human beings, and we will eat like civilized human beings."

He sat on the log beside the creature, raised the drumstick carefully, and took a delicate bite of the meat. When the hot juice burst into his mouth, it tasted so good and he was so hungry that he nearly set upon the chicken like an animal himself. But the giant was watching him attentively. Rinaldo had a responsibility to uphold. He chewed the bite thoroughly. He swallowed. He took a second bite.

His eyebrows drawn together in concentration, the giant raised the chicken and took a tiny, awkward nibble. He chewed with his mouth closed. He swallowed. He looked at Rinaldo.

"Very good," Rinaldo said. "Excellent."

And so their meal progressed, till the edge of their hunger dulled.

Once Rinaldo could put his mind to any subject beyond the simplest element of survival, his nascent curiosity about the giant grew. The man had many contradictions about him. He could speak, but behaved almost as if he were mute; though he was uninstructed, he was highly intelligent. He was willing, even eager, to learn, but he had passed his entire life without learning most of what Rinaldo considered essential. The more Rinaldo thought about the giant, the more reasons he found to be intrigued.

"Correct me if I'm wrong," Rinaldo said, "but I would guess you've lived for quite a time on your own."

The giant hesitated, as he always did before making the decision to speak. He touched his chest.

"Alone," he said.

"What about your parents? Your family?"

The giant shook his head.

"Perhaps you're lucky," Rinaldo said. "Family can be an awful trial. They think you were visited upon them as a punishment, or as a gift to do with as they please. Why, my friend, just think—you might have been worked to death like a plough horse, or kidnapped into slavery for the amusement of some eastern prince. Yes, that happens!" Rinaldo reacted to the giant's expression of disbelief. "I've heard of it any number of times. A pretty girl, or a pretty boy, or one of us who is . . . unusual. Snatched away in the night and traded for gold. That's what a family will do for you."

The giant shook his head again. "No family," he said. "No friend."

His voice, so low and harsh, made his emotions difficult to detect, but Rinaldo heard the sadness.

"No friend? Didn't you ever have a friend before?"

"They make friend. . . . She hate me."

" 'She,' eh? You and I . . . we're bound to have a little trouble in that line. It's a question of choosing properly, though, you see." Rinaldo tried to make sense of what the giant had said. If he had no friend, no family, then who were "they"? And what did he mean, *they* had *made* a friend? Some intrigue, or some cruel joke. . . . Given the giant's lack of learning, Rinaldo wondered how much, if anything, he knew about the most basic human interactions. Rinaldo's own knowledge was a curious combination of information gleaned in the gutter, expertise acquired when he had served one of the most accomplished courtesans in Europe, and personal experience. He suspected that the giant had no personal experience, he would have been willing to bet that he had never worked for a courtesan, and he doubted that the giant had ever had the benefit of childhood gutter discussions, of listening to the braggadocio, misinformation, and downright lies of boys a few years his senior.

"Tell me about the friend," he said. "Was she . . ." He hesitated, not quite sure how to broach the subject with any delicacy. ". . . like you?"

The giant nodded. "Like me."

Even a giantess might be frightened of a giant, if she were equally untaught, Rinaldo thought.

"What makes you think she hates you?"

The giant stared at the ground. "See me. Scream."

Rinaldo laughed. "My friend, I do believe you've confused hate with—something else. Perhaps fear, but more likely a sense of duty. Women are taught that sort of thing, or they are taught nothing at all. It causes no end of confusion, for them, for us. And it's true, they bear most of the risks. You have to understand. . . ." He saw that the giant did not understand, at all. One more thing for Rinaldo to explain. "Never mind that for now. Take it from me. I've been under a few petticoats in my day—caused a few screams of one sort or another, too. But it usually ended well. Why, once in a while you'll meet a woman who will scream just to see what effect it will have. My guess is that you gave up too easily."

The giant listened attentively, but with such a doubtful expression that Rinaldo wondered if he had comprehended one word in three.

"Beautiful," the giant said sadly.

"She was beautiful?"

The giant nodded.

Rinaldo tried not to smile. He did not want to hurt his new friend's feelings. He tried not to laugh. But he could not help but wonder what he would consider beautiful.

He burst out in an uncontrollable chuckle. The giant looked at him questioningly, and Rinaldo tried to remain serious.

"If she is anything like you," he said, "I shouldn't wonder if she were the loveliest creature on earth."

He started to laugh again, but the giant nodded with great solemnity.

"Beautiful," the giant said.

Rinaldo felt a little ashamed of himself for laughing.

"I'm glad you told me about her," he said. "No one can know a man, without knowing his dream."

That, the giant understood. "Dream," he said softly.

"Everybody has one." Rinaldo patted his chest. "It's the key to everything."

Chapter 4

The fire in the library hearth burned to ash and coals. Charles Frankenstein barely noticed the autumn morning's chill. He pored over the litter of books and papers on the table, planning Eva's lessons. He had never undertaken to educate a child before: he thought of her as a preternaturally bright child. She learned at a great rate. Charles would almost have preferred to proceed more slowly, but Eva would not stand for it. So he spent the day teaching her, and the night preparing her lessons. Already she could read, though her vocabulary was as yet insufficient to permit full comprehension. But that would come.

The door to the library swung open with such force that the heavy oak banged against the wall. Charles did not even raise his head. He marked a passage of Ovid.

"Charles!"

A hand clamped down on his shoulder and shook him roughly. He looked up, blinking. His eyes had been focused on the printed word so long that his vision blurred.

"At least you haven't lost your hearing!" Clerval said. "Your mind, perhaps, but not your hearing. Come with me."

"No, I have too much work to do—Eva will be awake soon, and we must begin again—"

William raised him forcibly to his feet. "Come with me, I said."

Charles found himself too fatigued to resist. He shivered from the cold.

"I must build up the fire," he said. "Eva—"

"Eva is asleep. You were closeted with her till three o'clock this morning—reading Thucidides! In the original!" William propelled him from the library and into the main hall. "Is that your idea of how to behave with a beautiful young woman in the middle of the night?"

"She's like a child, William—she has a child's facility with languages. But how long she'll retain the ability—"

"How long will she retain her patience, which must be that of a saint?"

"You don't understand her at all. Or me, for that matter."

"I understand that you're obsessed, and that your obsession is killing you." He threw Charles's riding cloak to him and picked up his own.

"What's this?" Charles said.

"You're further gone than I thought." William fastened his cloak and wrapped Charles's cloak around his friend's shoulders.

"I can't force you to eat. I can't force you to sleep. But I can force you to get some fresh air."

Charles had so severely depleted his strength with work that he could not prevent William's leading him from the castle. In the courtyard, Jan stood holding two horses.

"You keep an excellent stable, my friend," William said. "You do these beasts an injustice by never riding them."

"I have no time for play!"

"I don't intend to let you back inside until you've ridden out for at least half an hour. And your housekeeper will never let you in until she is convinced you've partaken of the excellent breakfast she has packed. Will you mount, or must I throw you bodily into the saddle?"

Charles thrust his foot into the stirrup and clambered onto his horse's back.

"Very well," he said unwillingly. "You give me no choice, so I will ride. But I warn you, William, if anything goes awry while I am gone—"

Laughing, William sprang onto his horse's back and spurred the animal into a run. Charles's mount took out after him. The clatter of horseshoes on cobblestones gave way to the thud of hooves on clay as the two horses raced down the lane.

On the other side of the meadow, William brought his horse back to a walk. Charles pulled up beside him, his mount prancing and blowing, unwilling to stop. The ride was beginning to dispel the deep chill from Charles's bones, and even his anger abated. It did feel good to be out in the light and air.

Though the west threatened rain, the sky overhead was clear and bright. The horses topped a rise and stopped for a moment. Charles looked out over the ancestral estate of the Frankensteins—*his* estate. At times he still did not believe he had gone from a childhood of poverty to this.

"Eva would like to see it. . . . Perhaps she is ready for her first experience of the world."

"Oh, 'Eva'!" William exclaimed. "I ride all the way up this wretched mountain with barely the shirt on my back to make certain you haven't burned your house down around your ears, and what's my reward? Thanks? No! For days on end I am ignored. When I am not ignored, I am assaulted by 'Eva, Eva, Eva'!"

"I believe you're jealous," Charles said.

"Jealous? I? I'm concerned for your health."

"I cannot spend my life carousing."

"Cannot? Of course you can. You have more money than

you could spend in a lifetime, and the freedom to do with it as you will. What you mean to say is, you will not."

"As you please, William. But I think you spend altogether too much time at play. Your friends—"

William looked at the sky as if in supplication. "Spare me, Charles. If you intend to inflict more criticism of Lord Byron on me, I must tell you I'd rather hear about your patient."

"She's extraordinary, William! She gives me new insight into the development of human intelligence. At first she had no self-control at all. The tantrums—"

"I well remember," William said dryly, recalling a recent morning when violent shouts sent him leaping from his bed, afraid that brigands had set upon the castle. Eva, tired and hungry after an entire night under Charles's tutelage, refused to look at another book or map or paper until someone gave her food. William reflected that under such circumstances he would have had a tantrum long since.

He dismounted beside a stone wall, tethered his horse, and unfastened the saddlebags. He spread their breakfast out on the sun-warmed rock. Charles followed with barely a pause in his narrative. A cloud passed before the sun.

"But in only a short time, she saw that tantrums had no effect in getting her what she wanted. I am permitting her to discover civilized behavior by means of the Socratic dialogue. My questions lead her inexorably to the truth, which she has found within herself."

"Mrs. Baumann's methods have nothing to do with her progress, I suppose."

"Mrs. Baumann," Charles said, "does not appreciate the more delicate aspects of the learning process."

"What about the more delicate subjects of the learning process?" William asked. "Have you taught your . . . patient . . . nothing but table manners and the alphabet? Tell the truth, Charles. You've taught her nothing at all about men and women?"

"The relation of the sexes does not yet concern us. She's still a child, in almost every sense of the word—and I'm losing patience with your Oriental morals in *that* regard. She is not even aware of herself as a sexual creature."

"I thought you were employing the Socratic method," William said sarcastically. "This sounds to me more like the Platonic."

"You have no imagination!"

"That isn't what you said in Paris. You abused me with precisely the opposite accusation."

"Can't you see that she's destined for a new kind of love —the love of equals?"

"You'll teach her about the love of equals, will you?"

"Love is the highest form of human communication, William. Therefore it is fitting that love be the last thing I teach her."

William laughed. "When your statue, like Pygmalion's, comes to life."

Angry, Charles stood up. "Go ahead and laugh!" he cried. "But one day she will astonish you!"

He grabbed his horse's reins.

"My dear Frankenstein," Clerval said, still laughing, "I only hope she doesn't astonish *you.*"

In a fury, Charles flung himself onto his horse and galloped back toward the castle. He had been too long away.

Charles had returned to the castle, thrown the reins of his horse to Jan, and set Eva to her lessons by the time he heard Clerval's horse jog into the courtyard. His anger at his oldest friend erupted again, but he fought it down. William's boots thudded on the stone tiles of the entry hall. Charles rose to go speak to him.

"What is this?" Eva said, pointing to a woodblock print in her book of fables.

Charles returned his attention to Eva, completely forgetting about William. He joined Eva.

"What does it say?" he asked.

She spelled out the words.

" 'The Lion is (beyond dispute) allow'd the most majestic brute.' " She traced the picture with one finger. "Lion," she said.

"Excellent!" Charles exclaimed. "Excellent, Eva!"

She favored him with a brilliant childlike smile and bent over the book again. He turned to her next lesson, on the principles of the prism. He let the angled glass faces throw bands of multicolored light onto the walls.

When he glanced up again, Eva sat curled in the chair, her bare feet dangling over the arm, her long, graceful, muscular leg exposed. Charles tried to speak to her, but suddenly and inexplicably found his mouth dry.

He flung the prism across the room. It exploded into tiny shards. Eva jumped, terrified.

"Sit upright!" Charles said, more angrily than he had intended. "Apply yourself! When we study, when we learn, we do a serious thing. It is knowledge that makes us human."

Eva met his glare directly, questioning his anger. She swung her feet to the floor, gathered the gown around her, and placed the book flat on the table. With a final curious quirk of one eyebrow, she bent over her book again.

Charles clenched his trembling hands, rose abruptly, and threw a log on the fire.

"Charles."

He started.

William stood in the library entrance, still wearing his riding cloak.

"I think it best that I go back to town."

The rainclouds had sped in to darken the afternoon. A sensible traveler would ask to stay till morning; a civilized host would insist upon it. Yet Charles could not bring himself to oppose William's plan.

"You are right," he said. "It *would* be best."

William nodded coldly. A few more words would break their friendship forever. William looked over Charles's shoulder at Eva; the single glance was almost enough to ignite Charles's temper again.

"Do not overwork yourself, my friend," William said. He strode from the house. His horse's hooves clattered in the courtyard; and he was gone.

I open the heavy carven doors and enter the church, my knapsack on my back. Inside, I stop, overwhelmed by the play of light as it passes through stained glass and glints from gold and flows over polished wood. As if I could catch the light and carry it away with me, I extend my hand into a multicolored shaft and watch the hues move across my skin, changing color and intensity.

"Here, you!"

The abrupt voice startles me. A small man—I suppose he might not be small by human standards, but all men are small to me; he is larger than Rinaldo, and he looks well-fed —hurries toward me, frowning.

A sharp poke in my shoulder is a signal. I obey it, backing up. But after a few steps I bump gently into a box attached to the wall behind me, and must stop.

"What do you want?" The small man sounds angry. He stops some paces from me when he realizes my size, but he does not scream and run like so many other humans do. He straightens and arranges his garments, preening his gold-embroidered robe as a pigeon preens his breast feathers.

"Please . . ." Words hurt my throat. I wish Rinaldo had agreed to ask in the church for food, instead of insisting that I do it.

"What?" The priest is angry at being interrupted, annoyed at my inarticulateness.

"Please," I say again, but he gives me no time to continue.

"State your business, man!"

"Hungry." My ugly voice rasps through the quiet chamber. I can hardly bear to hear it.

"Hungry?"

"Want food," I whisper. If Rinaldo could eat acorns, I would not have to be here.

"Food? I have no food here."

"Money? Money for food?" Rinaldo has tried to explain the concept of money to me, but I find it difficult to grasp.

The priest is nodding, but it is not a gesture of agreement. It is of understanding and disapproval. His mouth turns down in a frown.

"Oh, so that's it," he says, still nodding. "Money for food. I see. What do you suppose the world would be, if every beggar could walk into a church and get his living just by asking for it?"

Rinaldo said that if we came into the church, they would give us food. My stomach growls even louder as I realize that my friend was wrong. Rinaldo said churches represent love. He said the people who lived inside them loved their fellow men.

My pack moves against my back. Perhaps Rinaldo will appear now, and explain to the priest about love, or at least about sharing, which is I think an altogether more useful concept. But Rinaldo remains hidden.

"Hungry," I say hopelessly. Not being human, I do not deserve their love.

"I shouldn't wonder," the priest says haughtily. "Those

who *will* not work *will* not eat—and that, my son, is part of God's plan." He smiles at me; I do not understand why. "It would be no charity to fiddle with the wisdom of the Lord."

The movements in my pack cease, and a second poke, this time in my side, signals me again. Rinaldo has tested me, and found me wanting.

"Thank you," I whisper, backing out of the priest's august presence.

He smooths his robes again.

"You will thank me more and more as time goes by. Wisdom weighs more than gold, in the end. Truth tastes better than bread."

Perhaps he is correct, but bread tastes better than acorns, and right now I would be grateful for an acorn.

Rinaldo remained concealed in the sack the giant carried until he could see through the peephole that the church was out of sight. The giant trudged down the road, discouragement in his step. Rinaldo opened the top of the sack and clambered onto the giant's shoulder, jingling in his pocket the coins he had purloined from the poor box.

"Thank you, dear priest," he said happily, "thank you, thank you, thank you." He practically sang. He jumped up and stood on the giant's shoulder. From his vantage point, he could see the slowly swinging sign of a tavern. "Ale, ho!" he cried, urging the giant forward. "Dead on! Steer straight, sir, steer straight!"

Rinaldo pushed open the door of the tavern, strode inside, and gave the place the once-over.

It was everything he had expected: dark and smoky and heavy with the odor of stale beer. Two barrels and a plank formed the bar. But it was warm, a side of beef dripped sizzling fat into the fire, and surely the barrels ranged against the far wall held enough beer to slake Rinaldo's thirst. It should not take more than a few of them.

Rinaldo's eyes became more accustomed to the dim light. He could hardly miss the tavernkeeper's edgy glare. The other men at the bar turned and leaned arrogantly back on their elbows, inspecting him.

"Here, look," one said. "We've got a runt among us."

The tavernkeeper had a stronger reaction. He crossed himself.

"Clear out, you little devil," he said. "I don't want none of your lot in here, giving us the evil eye." He made a sign against the curse.

"He ain't no devil," another of the men said. "He ain't got no horns. I heard tell of pygmies, he must be one o' them."

"Pygmies got horns too."

"Horns or no horns!" the tavernkeeper yelled. "I don't—"

The giant walked through the doorway.

The tavern fell silent.

Rinaldo kept a straight face. He walked to the bar, thoroughly enjoying the spectacle of the tavernkeeper, who stared openmouthed at the giant. The formerly belligerent patrons turned back to their flagons of ale. The giant stopped beside Rinaldo and gazed mildly around.

"You'll be drinking, will you?" The tavernkeeper's voice quivered, but the immediate danger of the giant frightened him more than the hypothetical danger of Rinaldo's evil eye.

"*We* will be drinking," Rinaldo said.

The giant leaned down, picked him up, and set him easily on the bar.

"Two pints of ale, sir." Feeling most magnanimous, Rinaldo placed a silver piece on the bar. The tavernkeeper served them. Rinaldo grabbed his mug. The ale tasted so good that he downed it in a single draught.

Before Rinaldo finished, the giant was already gazing unhappily into his empty mug. For him, a pint of ale was a bare, intriguing taste.

"Another pint for me, sir," Rinaldo said to the tavernkeeper. "And something more capacious for my friend. Fill him a pail!"

Rinaldo drank his second pint almost as quickly as the first, but the giant lifted his brimming milk pail in both hands and drank the ale as if it were a pint. The onlookers gasped. The giant delicately licked the foam from his lips.

"Another pint!" Rinaldo cried. "And another pail!" The onlookers gasped. Rinaldo ignored them.

After one swallow from his third pint of ale, he felt as if one more sip would explode him like a shaken beer keg. But the giant lifted his pail in both fists and gulped his ale. He flung down the empty pail, dejected.

Suddenly his eyes went out of focus. He swayed backward, forward, backward—and crashed flat to the floor.

Rinaldo leaped to the ground. His knees buckled. He staggered, but kept his feet. He squinted at the giant. Giants. Two giants.

"When did you get a brother?" he said. "I'd've thought one of you would be enough for any family." He sat beside the giant and patted his massive chest. "You're quite right," he said. "It's time for sleep. Innkeeper! A room! Beds! Fresh sheets! We've earned 'em, and we can pay!"

"You'll get what you've earned," the tavernkeeper said, and Rinaldo smiled up at him. He was not such a bad fellow after all, once one got to know him.

"Get up, friend giant," Rinaldo said. The giant did not move. The tavernkeeper tied a length of rope around his ankles. He hardly breathed. His head spinning, Rinaldo climbed onto his chest and listened for his heartbeat. "Oh, woe!" he cried. "Woe, oh, woe, he's dead!" The rope tightened, dragging the giant toward the doorway. "He's dead, good sir, he's dead—no fault of your fine brew, I'm sure."

"Good riddance," the tavernkeeper said.

Rinaldo beat his fists on the giant's chest. "Good night, sweet giant!" he cried. "And flights of tavernkeepers sing thee to thy rest."

The rope tightened and pulled, sagged and loosened, and the giant proceeded in a series of jerks, like a ship with a quartering sea.

"Sail on, oh ship of sorrow!" Rinaldo began to feel seasick.

"Drive 'em, then! Drive 'em!" The rope tightened again and the giant slid out into the street, with Rinaldo swaying astride. The horses hitched to the other end of the rope dug in and pulled. They dragged the giant up a splintery ramp into the bed of a hay wagon. The driver hitched the horses to the wagon, jumped up into the seat, and grabbed the reins. Shouting and wailing, the spectators followed the wagon.

"Yes, weep!" Rinaldo shouted. "For I, who knew him best, say he was a paragon of larceny, a prince of balderdash . . . and if he lived he would render into mincemeat—into pies and pieces of pies!—anyone who dared to challenge what I say!" He started to stand up, the better to declaim the funeral oration. Halfway to his feet he thought better of the endeavor. He sat back down again, but continued his harangue.

"I tell you, he was the tiniest of giants, the smallest of titans—he was a pelican! A noble hedgehog of a man!"

The wheels echoed on the planks of a bridge. His head spinning, Rinaldo caught one glimpse of rushing water before the wagon turned and tilted. He tumbled over the railing.

The river closed over him with a cold and shocking splash. He struggled to the surface, gasping and choking. The giant splashed into the river nearby. Rinaldo went under again, and clawed his way back to air.

"That should sober you up!" one of the villagers yelled from the safety of the bridge, and spat after them.

"I can't swim!" Rinaldo cried. He snatched for a floating twig, a branch, the air. The villagers laughed and jeered. Rinaldo recognized the sounds he had earlier taken for lamentation.

As he started to go down for the third time, he heard a great gasp and splashing and saw to his joy that the giant had revived from his premature death. The giant struggled and floundered in the water.

Rinaldo waved and screamed. "I can't swim! I'm drowned! I'm done for! I'm sunk!"

He reached toward the air.

"I—" He looked down. "I'm standing up to my shoelaces in *mud.*"

The giant close behind, Rinaldo turned and scrambled up the bank. When the villagers saw their entertainment escaping, they snatched up stones and flung them. Running and dodging, Rinaldo and the giant escaped into the trees.

Rinaldo staggered down the road. He almost wished one of those stones had hit him. It would have put him out of his misery. Next to him, the giant walked very slowly, carefully putting one foot down and steadying himself before he raised his other foot.

The giant's massive hands covered his temples, his forehead, his eyes. Every time he took a step he had to part his fingers so he could see the road.

"Head," he said.

Rinaldo groaned and grabbed the top of his head. "Don't say that word!" Gingerly he lowered his hands. His head stayed more or less where it was. "And the pain," he said, "is not the worst of it. It's the remorse. Oh, bitter, bitter remorse. Is not drinking a sin?"

"Head," the giant said, not understanding.

"And does not sin lead to repentance, repentance to remorse—bitter, bitter remorse. There's a lesson in this!" He looked sternly at the giant. "And I hope to God I never learn it!"

He started to laugh. He sat down in the middle of the road, possessed by an hysterical fit of giggles, as the giant looked on perplexed.

Chapter 5

In the days after William Clerval left Castle Frankenstein, Charles dedicated himself entirely to Eva's education. During William's visit, Charles had resented every minute his old friend kept him away from her. Now, though, Charles missed the opportunity for adult conversation; and when on occasion Eva drove him to distraction, he cursed himself roundly for sending William away. Yet he persuaded himself that he was glad William had gone. Now that he had no guest to waste his time, he could devote every waking minute, and most of his dreams, to Eva.

She progressed rapidly. Though she retained surprising gaps in her knowledge, her grasp of language strengthened with each hour. Her hesitancy in movement gave way to assurance and grace. Even the scars on her wrists had faded to mere shadows. Her eyes, though—the lightning in her eyes never completely vanished. Charles could have spent the rest of his life gazing into her eyes.

He flung the thought from his mind as he flung the bedclothes from his body.

The bright morning brought a patch of autumn sun to his bedroom. He shaved hurriedly and dressed. He begrudged the time it took him to shave, and indeed only bothered because Mrs. Baumann had pointed out, with some asperity, that he was setting a poor example for Eva, "the wild little vixen." Mrs. Baumann had not changed her original opinion of Eva, but took the pragmatic attitude that if she were responsible for Eva's behavior, then Eva would behave.

Hearing shouts from Eva's room, he sighed. His patient and his housekeeper were in the midst of one of the battles of their perpetual war. He tied his neck-cloth haphazardly and hurried to the adjacent room.

"To the devil with you, you spoiled brat!"

"What's wrong, Mrs. Baumann?"

Eva wore a new dress that was only half buttoned. Her hair hung loose and she clenched her fists at her sides.

"Milord! It's not proper—"

"Never mind that. What's the matter?"

"She won't wear her frock!"

"Is that true, Eva?" Charles asked.

Eva plucked at the buttons. "Why can't I wear my robes?"

"Because it isn't proper for a young woman to go out in society wearing nothing but a scholar's gown."

"Why must I go out in society?"

"Because you'll be lonely if you don't meet other people."

"Why don't you meet other people?"

"I do. But I've been using all my time to help you, since you came to live with us. That will change soon."

"Why don't you want to help me anymore?"

"I do, Eva—"

"Milord!" Mrs. Baumann said. "She still won't wear her dress!"

"And one of the things I must help you with is learning to wear proper clothes," Charles said.

"Why is it so uncomfortable?"

"Why, it fits you perfectly, you ungrateful little minx," Mrs. Baumann said, "Didn't milord have a seamstress come all the way—"

"Mrs. *Baumann,*" Charles said. "Eva, it's only uncomfortable because you aren't used to it."

"Why is it so tight? Why does it have so many buttons? Why is it so long and full that I can hardly walk? Why do I have to wear so many things under it?"

"Because . . ." Charles had no good answers to any of her questions. "Because it's the fashion, I suppose, just like, oh, stovepipe trousers instead of breeches."

"Why?"

"Because—" he said with asperity.

Charles stopped when he saw the quick upward twitch of Eva's lips. She turned away, hiding her face in her hands to conceal her giggling.

"All right, my clever child," Charles said, hardly able to keep from laughing himself. "You've had your game. Now button your frock, and let us go to breakfast."

"But it *is* tight, and it *does* have too many buttons, and it *is* too long and full to walk in," Eva said. "I will wear stovepipe trousers!"

Mrs. Baumann gasped in horror.

"No," Charles said.

"But why?"

"Because it isn't proper."

"Why?"

"Because young ladies don't wear trousers."

"But I am not 'young ladies.' I am Eva."

"And Eva will wear her dress!"

"Why?"

"Because I want you to!" Charles shouted, completely out of patience.

Eva fell silent. "Then I will wear my dress," she said finally, and set to buttoning the last buttons.

Charles descended to the main floor. A few minutes later,

Eva followed. Her stately glide contradicted her assertion that her dress was too clumsy to walk in.

"Now, that isn't so bad, is it?" he asked, and led her into the breakfast room.

She fidgeted during breakfast, but only twice, and not at all after he reminded her to sit still. Then they repaired to the library. This morning he set her to reading out loud to him. He let himself dissolve into the sound of her strong, gentle voice.

"'And there beneath the tree, reclining . . .'" She paused. "What does it say: 'a tree'?"

"A tree! A tree is—" Charles always found himself most surprised when Eva lacked knowledge of ordinary objects. She had no more way of knowing intuitively what a tree was than she had of knowing the calculus. She had begun to learn the calculus; now was the time for trees. He drew a rough sketch and showed it to her.

She looked at it, puzzled.

"Oh, for God's sake," Charles said. He pointed out the window. "That's a tree."

Eva followed the direction of his gesture, and frowned.

"It is a window," she said.

"No, no!" He pointed again, then leaped to his feet. "This is ridiculous. Come with me."

Frankenstein threw open the front door.

The soft air and cool light burst upon Eva as powerfully as any storm.

Frankenstein turned and glanced back impatiently.

"Eva? Come along."

She ran down the stairs and onto the long rolling expanse of greenness that spread before the castle. It was deeper and softer, yet more irregular, than any carpet. It was surrounded by walls of darker green that reached above her head. She could see all the way into the sky! She spread her arms, as if to take the universe to herself and know it all, all at once.

Frankenstein stood beside a tall and complicated structure, brown and roughly cylindrical at the bottom, branched and covered with fluttery bits of red and yellow and orange at its top. Eva joined him. He slapped the brown part of the structure.

"This is a tree," he said. "We are under a tree."

The paper he showed me, Eva thought, was merely a map of a tree!

She put her hand on the tree's trunk. Its bark was rough and hard, yet somehow pleasant to touch, with edges of green softness. A leaf fell from a branch. She caught it in both hands and stroked it, wondering if the tree were breaking, wondering if she could put the leaf back.

"As a matter of fact," Charles said, "paper—books—are made out of trees."

"Books?" She placed her hands flat against the trunk of the tree and leaned close, listening. The tree whispered to her, hinting that it knew the secrets of the universe, secrets it would tell her if she could only listen carefully enough. "I hear books talking," she whispered. "Books in trees—" In her mind, she placed the image of the tree next to its sound, and next to the letters that formed its name. She smiled suddenly, seeing a pattern that pleased her. "Trees in books!"

"Yes," Charles said. "That's one way of putting it."

Eva gazed through the successive layers of leaves and branches. Here and there they parted just enough to permit a blue bit of sky to gleam through.

How could I have stayed indoors so long, she thought, when the whole, wild outside was calling to me?

"Look what I can do!" she cried.

She leaped to the lowest branch and scrambled into the tree. It welcomed her with its many arms and brushed her face with its soft leaves, scattering drops of water like the finest perfume across her face and hair. She remembered the alluring scent that had drifted through the open window on the first day of her awakening, almost the first thing she *could* remember.

"Eva!" Charles cried in horror. "No! No! Now, I tell you, you must not—Eva!"

She climbed higher and higher till the branches bent under her weight, and she knew if she climbed higher she would injure this great, complex being that embraced her and bathed her in its secret whispers.

"Eva! Get down!"

She barely heard him. She was many times her height above the ground. She parted the branches and looked out into the world.

From here she could see beyond the hedge. She gasped at the sheer unimaginable size of the outdoors. In one direction, the world stretched farther than she could see. In the other, it ended in a wall—but such a wall! The jagged, white-peaked top touched the sky. She wondered how anyone had built it.

The wind took her hair and ruffled it around her face, entwining it with the branches of the tree as if they could all become a single creature: Eva, the tree, the wind. She laughed again, exhilarated.

The tree shook. Far below, Frankenstein clung desperately to the lowest branch of the tree.

"Eva!" he shouted. "Come down at once!"

She could barely hear him over the seductive whispering of the tree and the wind.

"I can see the world!" she cried. "Everywhere! It's big! The world is big!"

She swayed with the branches, around and around, till she grew dizzy—

I trudge down the road to Budapest, footsore and tired, wishing the journey at an end. Suddenly the world spins around me. I stumble to a halt, swaying, possessed by a feeling of dizziness, joy, and abandon.

Rinaldo, at my side, stops and regards me strangely. I can barely hear him through the whispering in my ears.

"What's this, what's this? Are you tired? Are you ill?"

I struggle to respond, with my painful, crippled voice. My head is spinning, like a bird soaring into an updraft—

—Eva stopped and stood laughing till her balance returned. She laughed, yet tears ran down her face.

"Eva!"

Frankenstein's voice was hardly louder than the whisper of the trees. Eva looked down. Far below, Frankenstein clutched the tree's trunk. His face had lost all color and he seemed about to swoon. Frightened for him, Eva scrambled down. The branches scraped her legs and feet and caught at her full skirt, as if unwilling for her to depart.

"I will come back," she whispered. "I will come back."

She reached Frankenstein.

"What is wrong?" she said. "Come higher, it is beautiful."

"No," he said. "You might fall. Come down. Come down immediately."

"Very well," she said, disappointed. She would not fall. She leaped to the ground. "I am down."

He opened his eyes. Clutching the tree trunk, he slid awkwardly down. He hardly loosened his grip when he finally stood on solid ground.

"I was afraid you would fall," he said.

Suddenly he swooned.

Frightened for him, Eva knelt beside him.

"Frankenstein? What is wrong? Are you asleep?"

He lay quiet and still on the grass. She sat beside him till he revived, then helped him into the castle.

Rinaldo watched with concern as the giant staggered and swayed.

"Are you tired?" he said. "Are you ill?"

"Head goes around," the giant whispered. "Like a bird."

Rinaldo grasped the giant's hand, fearful of his health, or even his sanity. But as suddenly as the fit had come on him, it stopped. He straightened and smiled down at his small friend.

"Stops," he said.

"How very odd," Rinaldo said, not quite able to conceal his concern. "Perhaps we'd better stop for the night. A half a day's walk brings us to Budapest, and we want to reach it in daylight, don't we? Refreshed and renewed."

The giant made no objection.

"Budapest," he said, pronouncing the word carefully.

"It's nuts and cake to a couple of sharp fellows like us. Nuts and cake!"

Half a mile down the road they found a small abandoned building, like a gazebo, and there they camped.

While the giant collected fallen branches, Rinaldo took stock of their possessions. He brought out his needle and thread and mended a new rip in his only coat.

"Wretched villagers," he muttered. "No respect for a man's possessions. They might at least have checked for splinters before they pushed us off the bridge."

The giant dropped a vast armload of wood and hunkered down. Being dragged through the tavern, into the street, and into the wagon; being dropped off the bridge; swimming across the river, had not made much difference in the giant's appearance, but that was because his garments were already frayed and torn. As far as Rinaldo could tell, no one had ever made any attempt to mend the rents in the fabric.

"Give us your coat," he said.

Rinaldo showed him the needle to indicate what he planned. Uncomprehending, the giant took off his coat and gave it to Rinaldo. Then he watched in fascination. When Rinaldo had finished mending the first and largest tear, the giant drew his finger over the line of stitching and made a low sound of wonder.

Night fell while he finished the giant's coat, but the fire still gave light. Rinaldo dusted off the coat and inspected it.

"That'll do," he said. "Give us the shirt."

Making a strange sad noise deep in his throat, the giant shook his head and turned away.

"Give us the shirt, sir!" Rinaldo said. "I won't walk into Budapest with a man who's got rips in his shirt."

Staring at the ground, the giant slowly unbuttoned his shirt.

Here's an oversufficiency of modesty, Rinaldo thought.

But then the giant drew the shirt from his shoulders, revealing the awful scars on his back and chest.

"Oh, my . . ." Rinaldo repressed a curse, knowing that to react too strongly would further embarrass his friend. Yet he wished—no, he *needed*—to express some sympathy over the terrible flogging or brutal torture that the giant had endured. "Here is a man," he said, "that's been mistreated, once upon a time. It's no wonder, no wonder he keeps his story to himself."

The giant fed the fire and stared into the flames.

"Not . . . real man," he said. He drew his finger along a scar that crossed his chest and belly and disappeared beneath his belt.

Rinaldo blushed furiously, assuming the most obvious interpretation, and remembering some of the cruder jibes he had made to the giant.

"Stuff!" he said angrily. "Stuff and nonsense! I've been round the world a time or two and traveled with many men, for a long way or a short way—and I can't say I've ever found better company than I've had on this road. You're a man to reckon with, in my book. A man of virtues, sir!"

The giant raised his head. The gratitude in his face nearly broke Rinaldo's heart.

"Friend?" the giant said.

"I am proud to call you one. And I think . . . the time has come for you to have a name."

The giant shook his head. "No name."

"I don't ask for your real one!" Rinaldo said. If someone had treated him as the giant had been treated, neither would he give even a friend the smallest clue to his real identity. "I will give you a name. In Budapest, you'll need it."

"Give me . . . name?"

"Yes, sir."

The giant leaned eagerly toward him.

"What name?"

"Let me see," Rinaldo said, enjoying the giant's anticipation. "I think . . . Viktor."

"Viktor?" the giant said, hesitating over the pronunciation.

"Viktor. It means, 'he will win.' "

"Viktor," the giant said again.

"He will win—his heart's desire! Budapest is just the beginning, you see. When we've made our fortune, we'll go looking for our heart's desire. You'll go home with a lot of fancy things for your lady friend—*then* you'll see if she screams or not." It *was* possible, after all. A fortune could overcome any number of defects of face or form. But

Viktor's expression sobered abruptly at the mention of the lady, so Rinaldo quickly changed the subject. "I . . ." he said, "I have a dream too, you know."

"Dream?" Viktor asked.

"And since you told me yours, I'll tell you mine. It's not much of a dream, as dreams go. But I like it well enough."

"What?"

"Venice. I want to see Venice. 'I stood in Venice, on the Bridge of Sighs . . .' I haven't yet, of course, but someday I will see Venice."

"Vens?"

"All the streets are made of water!" Rinaldo exclaimed. "I want to see if it's really true. Streets made out of water. Just think . . . what if it *is* true?"

He glanced at Viktor, but he had not drawn the giant into his vision of a city floating in the water like a fantastical island. In a city whose streets were made of water, what other magical things might occur?

"Viktor," Viktor said.

Chapter 6

Eva allowed Hannah, the maid, to button her clothing for her. She could manage the odd, complicated fastenings herself, but Mrs. Baumann insisted that she needed help. Eva still wished Mrs. Baumann and Frankenstein had not taken away the comfortable scholar's gown.

"You should have a proper lady's maid, Miss Eva," Hannah said. "I can't understand why milord never got one for you. Doesn't he mind that your hair isn't never properly dressed? If I take the time to do it right, Mrs. Baumann will abuse me for neglecting my other work. You need someone to attend you all the time."

"I can comb my own hair, Hannah," Eva said. "And bathe myself. Why, I can even put on my own clothes. If you are being overworked, then I will insist that you not be forced to help me."

"Oh, no, Miss Eva, that isn't what I meant! I'd rather work half the night than give up tending to you. I only wish I could do it properly. I could, if they'd let me—I know what to do. I don't understand why milord doesn't want you to look your best. Could be he's afraid someone would come and steal you away from him, but now his sly-eyed friend has gone, who's he jealous of? And if he don't treat you right, who'd blame you if you found another to take you away and give you what you deserve?"

She paused, as if waiting for some response from Eva, but

as Eva felt thoroughly confused by what Hannah had said, she remained silent.

"It isn't like he can't afford a servant just for you, even if he won't have one himself. He will have the best of things—he even buys you silk for everyday." She touched the smooth sleeve of Eva's dress, and Eva noticed for the first time the difference between the clothes she wore and the rougher material of Hannah's dress and apron. "I'm frightened to touch your things, Miss Eva, for fear my nasty skin will snag them and ruin them."

Eva took Hannah's hands. Her skin was red and callused, her knuckles chapped from scrubbing, her fingernails as short and broken as Eva's had been when first she came here. But Eva's nails had grown out, and Hannah had filed and buffed them to perfect shiny ovals.

Hannah hid her hands beneath her apron.

"Don't look at them," she said. "They're ugly."

"You did this to my fingernails," Eva said, touching the smooth tip. "You said it was proper. So why do you not do it to your own?"

"Because I'm a maid, Miss Eva—and a scullery maid at that! I come to you still reeking of grease from the pots I scrub! When Mrs. Baumann sent me to you I thought you would slap me and send me back to the kitchen. You should have been insulted to be attended by such a one as me. Instead, you treated me kindly—I don't understand why, but I do know that if Mrs. Baumann caught me polishing my nails, she'd not treat me kindly. She'd beat me within an inch of my life for getting above myself."

"She will *not* beat you," Eva said. She opened a pot of lotion from her dressing table, scooped some out, and uncovered Hannah's hands. Hannah tried to pull away, but her heart was not in it. She let Eva rub the soothing lotion on her work-hardened skin. Still, she trembled.

"Mrs. Baumann—" she said.

"If Mrs. Baumann objects, you may tell her I ordered you to smooth your hands." She smiled. "So you do not 'snag and ruin' my clothing."

"I—I like taking care of you, Miss Eva. I like it when you talk to me. You never treat me like I'm nothing, and you never call me a stupid clapperdudgeon—"

"What," Eva said, "is a clapperdudgeon?"

"A fool," Hannah said. "A beggar."

"Why should I call you that, when you are neither?"

"Mrs. Baumann says I'm already the first, and she says I'd be the other if she hadn't taken me in as scullery maid. No doubt she's right, there's not much work for the likes of me. If I displease you, I'll have to go to the city and beg. Or worse, like as not."

"I'm sure you could never displease me, Hannah. But it troubles me, that you must work so hard while I sit idle—"

"Idle, Miss? You spend every day laboring over books and papers, hardly seeing the sun—your pretty eyes are all bloodshot when you finally go to bed."

"It does not seem like work to me. The time flies by so fast—I'll never have enough of it to learn everything I want to know. Frankenstein believes the same, I think, for whenever I ask to go outside again, he says we have too much to do."

"Even the Lord God rested on the seventh day!" Hannah said. "Milord should let you do as you please one day in seven. Why, even servants get half the Sabbath to ourselves!" She sighed. "Ah, Miss, that's our lot in life, whether we're maids or ladies. We must do as they say."

"I don't understand what you mean, Hannah. Who are 'we,' who must take orders, and who are 'they,' who have the right to give them?"

"Women and men, Miss Eva," Hannah said. "We are

weak, they are strong. We must submit our lives to their fancy—you know that, you understand that. It's God's will."

"I understand no such thing! That is ridiculous!"

"But, Miss Eva," Hannah said, perplexed, "you said yourself he would not even let you go outside. I must do as he says because he is my employer, and you must do as he says because you are his—"

She stopped.

"His what, Hannah?"

Her fair cheeks turning scarlet, Hannah looked at the floor. "I cannot say it, Miss Eva. Please forgive me! I never meant an insult, please don't tell milord I said such a thing! Please don't tell Mrs. Baumann!"

The young woman burst into tears.

"Don't cry, Hannah, it's all right. You gave me no insult, but I don't understand you." She put her arm around Hannah's shoulders and patted her awkwardly, not knowing how to comfort her. "I won't tell anyone, but please tell me what you meant."

"I cannot, I cannot." Hannah buried her face in her hands, sobbing convulsively. "Please don't send me away—"

"Never mind," Eva said. "Never mind. We won't speak of it anymore."

After Hannah went downstairs, Eva sat staring into her looking glass for some minutes. Much of what the young woman had said confused her; and some of it upset her.

"Eva?" Frankenstein threw open the door to her bedroom and strode in. "I've been waiting—it's time for your morning study."

"I would like to go outside again," Eva said.

"Yes, yes, of course," he said impatiently. "Perhaps this afternoon. Come to the library."

She rose and followed him downstairs.

He let her read what she pleased for half the morning. She enjoyed reading, but her thoughts wandered beyond the dark, book-lined room to the world outside.

Making her put aside her book, Frankenstein lectured her on the principles and details of the circulatory system. She listened with only half her attention.

"The heart, which is called the seat of the affections, is in fact a pump—it moves the blood into every region of the body, and back again. Dr. William Harvey . . ."

Eva thought of the tree and its whispers of freedom, of the smell of the wind and the taste of the air.

"Eva! Are you listening?"

"Yes."

"I don't believe you are."

She repeated the lesson to him, word for word.

He held up his hand to stop her. "I stand corrected. But you gave every appearance of being a thousand miles away."

"I do not wish to be a thousand miles away," she said. "I only wish to go outside."

"Perhaps later."

But after the midday meal, Frankenstein took her straight back to the library. Far from letting her go outside, he closed the curtains so she could not even see the sunlight. When she objected he told her it was necessary, and showed her a machine made of wire brushes and cranks. From it protruded two silver rods, one bearing a small globe on its tip. He grasped the crank and turned it.

"Aether is a medium like our atmosphere, but more subtle, filling the interstices of the air. It is the aether which transmits the electric charge—"

A thin blue spark sizzled from the globe to the rod, sparking and snapping. Frankenstein turned the crank faster. The spark crackled louder and arched above the globe. Eva stepped back automatically, frightened for no reason she could think of.

"Don't be afraid, Eva." He chuckled. "It won't hurt you."

"I'm not afraid!" she said, angry at herself for being afraid, angry at him for laughing at her. "I want to go outside. I *will* go outside!"

She stormed from the library, slamming the door behind her.

The tree whispered to her, speaking of all the places she had never seen. She leaned against the trunk, pressing her forehead to the rough bark.

"Eva," Frankenstein said, "come back inside."

"No."

He stood behind her in silence for a very long time. His anger made her unhappy.

Why do I want so much to please him? she thought.

"Very well," he said. "Come with me."

She shook her head, feeling miserable and confused.

"Not back inside, my little vixen," he said. Far from sounding angry, he sounded mischievous, as he did when he had something new to teach her. "You're right, I've made you work much too hard. Come along. Trust me."

She followed him through the gates to the inner courtyard, thence to the stables, where she had never been.

The rich animal odor fascinated her. She had watched from her window as the great beasts clattered across the cobblestones. When they moved about in their stalls, their hooves rustled softly on the straw.

"Jan!" Frankenstein called.

His groom appeared from the back of the stable.

"Yes, milord?"

"Saddle the black, and the gray mare."

"The mare, milord? But—"

"Do as I say, Jan!"

"Yes, milord."

Eva watched, enthralled. Jan saddled the two horses. The gray horse champed at the bit. She had a wild eye and a glossy coat, and she swiveled her ears back and forth, listening. Eva reached out hesitantly and touched the mare's shoulder. The glossy dappled coat quivered beneath her hand. Eva stroked the mare's neck more firmly. It was warm and sleek and smooth as silk. The horse watched her sidelong and swiveled one ear toward her. Eva whispered wordlessly to the horse, as the tree had whispered to her.

Jan led the two horses into the courtyard. Eva touched the bridle, exploring the leather and brass with her fingers. The mare pranced and snorted. The warm fragrant breath brushed Eva's cheek. She stood before the gray horse and exhaled softly into her nostrils. The mare pricked both her ears forward and blew her breath out gently. Eva stroked her muzzle.

"Eva, be careful!" Frankenstein hurried to her side, grabbed the reins, and jerked down on the bit. The mare reared back. Her steel shoes rang on the cobblestones. "Perhaps I was wrong to choose this horse for you. She's very spirited—"

"No!" Eva said. "No, please, I will be careful."

"Very well. But we will just walk quietly around the courtyard for your first riding lesson."

He gave her a leg up and showed her how to hold the reins. The mare jerked her head upward against the pressure of the bit.

"Always be firm with a horse, and calm—never show fear," Frankenstein said. "Guide her with the reins, gently but with great conviction." Frankenstein turned away to mount his own horse.

The mare quivered between Eva's knees. Eva flung her

hands forward, giving the mare her head, and clamped her legs to the horse's sides. The gray mare sprang off her haunches into a headlong gallop.

"Eva!"

Eva knew the mare would stop if she asked it of her, but though she controlled the horse's power, she could not bear to restrain it.

The mare sped down the road, between the hedges, and into the world that Eva had only glimpsed from afar.

Frankenstein's horse careened after them, but the fierce gray mare widened the gap between them with every stride.

They raced down the rough, rutted road, the mare's hooves flinging mud and fallen leaves. The forest ended, and the path led out into rolling meadows. As if she knew Eva's mind, the horse turned off the road and galloped into a sloping field. The high grass whispered against her legs. Stone walls partitioned the field into squares, cutting Eva off from the top of the hill. The mare pounded toward the barrier, never faltering. Eva leaned close over the mare's neck, exhilarated.

"God in heaven, Eva, stop!" Frankenstein called, from far behind.

The gray mare soared over the solid stone wall, clearing it easily, and cantered to the top of the hill. There she stopped, head high and neck arched, blowing her breath out noisily in the joy of her speed and power. Eva, too, felt breathless. She stroked the mare's shoulder and whispered to her.

Frankenstein followed more slowly. His horse balked at the wall, nearly throwing him. He climbed the hill by a more roundabout path that made use of the gaps in the walls. Eva watched him approach. At first she thought he was angry and terrified, but as he came closer she decided she must be mistaken. He seemed rather paler than usual, but aside from that he remained composed.

He drew his horse up beside hers.

"I see," he said, "that you've got the feel of it."

Eva stroked her horse's neck again. The mare swiveled her ears back, listening, waiting for a word that would free her to run again.

"She knows what I want her to do," Eva said.

They crossed the ridge, riding more slowly now to let the horses breathe. The ground sloped upward again. Eva treasured every sensation: the wind touching her through the silk of her dress, the crisp living scent of the air, the countryside opening out around her, the sunlight and the clouds.

"How far can we go?" Eva said, knowing he would not say "Forever," but wishing that he could.

"As far as you like," he said, smiling. The pallor had left his face.

They passed beneath the heavy green branches of a pine forest that enclosed them with its spicy odor. After a time the forest ended. The path led above the tree line and over talus. The slope fell away sharply to one side. Eva rode close to the edge, looking into the valley below.

"Eva, come back—the edge is dangerous. The road might break away, the horse might shy."

"She will not shy," Eva said; but Frankenstein seemed so agitated that she guided the horse nearer the center of the path.

Around the next outcrop of rock, a ruined stone tower stood crumbling back into the mountainside. Beyond it, carved stones and granite crosses projected from the ground.

"What is that?" Eva asked.

"The ruins of the monastery of St. Carlov," Frankenstein said. "A very old and noble place."

"I want to go walk there."

"Very well," he said.

They dismounted and tethered the horses by the low stone wall. Just inside the entrance she hesitated. The whole place, the very stones of the earth, spoke to her. They whispered of incalculable times of searching and doubt. Frankenstein strode ahead into the sanctuary. Eva followed him. The sun poured light through the empty western windows. Eva looked up through the roofless tower, to the darkening sky. She touched her fingertips gently to the walls. Their history echoed through endless years.

"It feels . . . like your walls," she said.

"It was built at the same time, by the first Baron Frankenstein, many hundreds of years ago."

"Before you were born?"

Frankenstein smiled. "Long before that. The monks of St. Carlov sheltered the travelers who used this pass, but when a safer road was cut farther south, the travelers stopped coming and the monks moved on."

Beyond the tower, a second, more massive stone wall surrounded the carven stones and crosses.

"What is that?" Eva said.

"That is a cemetery, where all my family are buried."

She followed him into the enclosure. Inside, it was very quiet. A huge oak tree grew in silence in a sheltered corner. Even the stones stilled their ethereal whispering.

"My father is here," Frankenstein said. He pointed to a tall, rounded headstone. "He died . . . in the arctic." He turned away from that grave and gestured to another. "My grandfather . . . all of us."

"What is a cemetery?"

"It's where we all come, sooner or later. When we're dead. To the grave."

"What is 'dead'?" Eva asked.

"It's . . . sleeping. Sleeping forever. One day we go to sleep, and never wake up."

"I don't know if I could sleep that long," Eva said. She wondered if the silence of the place were because the trees and rocks had given up trying to speak to those who slept.

A small stone building stood to one side of the monastery. A dark entranceway led into it.

"And what's that?" Eva asked.

"That's the old crypt of St. Carlov's, where the monks are sleeping."

Eva wanted to see someone who could sleep forever. She strode into the passage.

"Don't—" Frankenstein said.

But she had already descended the stairs to the dank chamber. Condensation slicked the floor. The ceiling opened upward into a lantern, a stone structure pierced with holes to admit daylight. Vaults lined the windowless walls; bones filled the vaults and lay scattered around, disturbed by wolves or vandals.

Frankenstein stopped on the bottom stair.

"Come back up. It's not healthy here."

Eva bent down and picked up a rounded piece of bone. She turned it this way and that.

"What is this?" she asked.

"That was a monk."

She looked at it; she listened for its whisper. But it remained mute.

"This?"

"I've told you about bones," Frankenstein said, "and skulls."

"This was a man?" She turned it about in her hands, and suddenly it was staring at her with empty eyes. It had no nose, only a gaping hole. Its upper teeth were gapped and crooked, and it had no lower jaw. "This is what we look like, underneath our faces?"

"Yes."

Eva smiled at the skull.

"May I take it with me?"

"No. These bones were laid to rest here. This is where they belong."

Disappointed, Eva laid the skull down.

"Come along," Frankenstein said again. "It's nearly dark. It's time to go home."

Charles watched Eva approvingly at dinner that evening. They had both returned from the afternoon's ride splashed with mud. Eva had bathed—Charles smiled to himself: now she bathed willingly and with pleasure; a great change from her first bath—and put on a new gown. She had dressed her hair differently, as well. Her table manners were impeccable. He watched her hands, her long, dexterous fingers. Her nails had grown out. Her wrists showed only the barest trace of scars. She looked very much a lady.

Charles felt exceedingly proud of his creation.

Since they had wasted an entire afternoon that could have been spent on lessons, he questioned her about past readings. But his thoughts kept straying, and he had to force them back to intellectual exercises.

"St. Thomas Aquinas founded his system," Eva said, "on the philosophy of Aristotle. But he adopted—"

"Adapted," Charles said. "He adapted it."

"He *adopted* it for his own purposes and *adapted* it to the needs of the Church. I believe that's correct."

"It is," Charles said. "That's quite enough about Thomas Aquinas. What have you read today?"

"I have read *The Tempest,* by William Shakespeare."

"You've been reading that for a week," Charles said.

"I read it once, and now I am reading it again."

"Why?"

"Because," Eva said, "it puzzles me."

"What puzzles you?"

"Why Miranda goes with Ferdinand. Why she leaves Caliban."

"Caliban is a monster!" Charles said.

"But she knows him. Ferdinand is a stranger. He doesn't know about the island."

"But Ferdinand is young and beautiful—he's her future. She says it: 'O brave new world—'"

"'—that has such creatures in it. . . .'" Eva finished the quotation in a soft voice; Charles thought he heard a question in it.

"It's very simple," he said.

Eva nodded, more in thought than in agreement. Charles had it in mind to press the point, but before he could speak, Mrs. Baumann entered with the wine for the next course. Eva took her arm as she passed, and the housekeeper stopped, startled.

"Mrs. Baumann," Eva said, "this beef is very good, but you've cooked it too long."

"What!" Mrs. Baumann exclaimed. Her high complexion reddened further.

Charles tried to think of a way to deflect the storm he saw coming. He failed.

"You've made it dry and tough by cooking it too long," Eva said. "In all the books of cooking I've read—"

Mrs. Baumann jerked her arm from Eva's grasp and turned on Charles in a fury.

"Milord, I won't put up with this! Lectured on beef, am I?" She spun and pointed at Eva. "By *that?*"

Charles tried to keep from laughing, but here again he failed. Eva's spirit delighted him. She needed more challenge than verbal sparring with a housekeeper.

"Mrs. Baumann, I think the lady is ready for the wider world, don't you?"

"Ready to get her ears boxed, if she don't watch out!" She glared at Eva. "Cooked the beef too long!" She stormed out of the dining room, muttering, "She'd eat it raw if I let her."

Charles smiled at Eva, who watched Mrs. Baumann's departure with a curious frown. She turned toward Charles, waiting for him to explain.

"I think you are," he said. He nodded. "Ready."

With a cry of fear, Eva sat bolt upright in her bed. Light and sound crashed around her. Wind through the open casements whipped the bedcurtains and scattered rain against her face. She looked wildly about, seeking something she had lost and forgotten.

The door to her room slammed open and a wavering flame floated toward her.

"What is it, what's the matter, you wicked creature?"

"I—I rode to the monastery," Eva said. "I took . . ." She could hardly think, because of the thunder and the rain. "I took all my books with me, and now they're gone." She threw aside the bedclothes. "I must go back and fetch them!"

"Your books! You silly snip, you have no books. All the books are the Baron's."

The housekeeper pushed Eva back into bed.

"Besides, how could you have taken books to the monastery, on horseback? Lie still and be quiet, lest you wake milord. I'll get you a brandy to make you sleep."

She hurried away again, taking the candle with her.

The room fell into darkness, but a crackle of lightning flooded it with an eerie blue illumination. Eva slipped out of bed and hurried from the castle.

Rain pelted her, soaking her nightgown and plastering her hair to her cheeks. Its coldness invigorated her and cleared her mind. She knew she must return to the monastery to find what she had lost, before she lost it forever. She ran across the courtyard and into the stable. Frightened by the thunder, the horses stamped and snorted.

Eva threw open the door of her mare's stall. The gray horse sidled away, the white showing around her eyes, her ears swiveling forward and back.

"I need your help," Eva whispered. She stretched out her hand to the mare, who hesitated, then lipped at her palm. Eva put one hand on either side of the mare's muzzle and blew gently into her nostrils. The mare calmed. Eva grasped her mane near the withers and swung onto her bare back. She leaned forward and whispered again. Bridleless, saddle-less, alert to every touch of Eva's leg or hand, the gray mare bolted from the stall, through the stable, across the court-yard, and into the night.

Still half asleep, Charles Frankenstein ran through the freezing rain to the stable. Mrs. Baumann had rousted him from his bed with the news that Eva had disappeared, and all he could make of her hysterics was that Eva had said something about going to the cemetery. He quickly tacked up a horse and urged it, unwillingly, into the storm. The lantern swinging at his stirrup gave only a fleeting, untrust-worthy light. Sensing Charles's agitation and fear, the horse pranced and snorted at the thunder. Charles laid his whip along its flank and forced it to the road.

The rain soaked Charles to the skin. Darkness made the trail endless. In the pine forest, rain-heavy branches swept down and slapped his face. But when he left the forest, he became painfully aware of his vulnerability to the lightning. The horse picked its way between and through the half-ruined stone walls. Lightning hit nearby, so close he could smell its discharge. Charles's fear for Eva overcame his ter-ror for himself, and he spurred the horse on.

He saw Eva's horse, unsaddled, unbridled, wild-eyed and demonic. He imagined that the girth had snapped, the saddle fallen, and that Eva lay dying in the darkness. But then he saw her standing among the stones of the cemetery, surrounded by an unearthly light. The wind whipped her soaked nightgown around her ankles and tangled her hair wildly around her head. He leaped off his horse and ran toward her. Her gaze darted from one stone to the next, desperately, as if she were searching for something without which she could not survive.

She thrust out her hand to fend him off. The eerie glow picked out the livid scars on her wrist. He stopped.

"Who am I?" she cried.

"You're Eva!" Charles said. "You're my ward!" He could barely hear his own voice above the tumult of the storm.

She pointed at the headstones—at the headstone of his father, who died so young and so strangely.

"Where is *my* father?"

"He's not here. No one knows who your father is." He tried to take her hand, but she stepped away.

"Where did I come from?"

"From Brucor," he said, just as he had always planned it. "From Brucor, where you were found."

"I want to go *home!* To *my* home!"

A bolt of lightning crashed down upon the oak tree. Eva screamed. Half-blinded, Charles stumbled forward to catch her as she fell. He carried her to his horse, which stood shivering and spraddle-legged, head down, bloody froth dripping from its bit. He passed the remains of the oak tree. It had thrived for centuries in a place where its growing should have been impossible, but in an immeasurable instant, the lightning had destroyed it. It reminded him of a passage in a book he had once read: "It was not splintered by the shock, but entirely reduced to thin ribbands of wood. I never beheld anything so utterly destroyed."

Carrying Eva across his saddlebow, Charles rode slowly back to the castle. The thunder and lightning faded and ceased, but the chill rain came down even harder. Giving the horse its head, Charles bent over his ward, concerned for her life and sanity. She did not stir, but he found her pulse. He wrapped his coat around them both.

Charles heard a sound. He turned. The gray mare followed, docile as a pony.

As they entered the pine forest, the lantern on his stirrup fluttered and died. He had to trust the horse to take them home. It plodded tiredly along the trail, head down, ears flattened against the rain. Once it left the path and stood shivering, tail turned to the wind, but Charles jerked up on the reins and spurred it onward.

Finally they reached the castle. His horse plodded into the courtyard, the gray mare close behind. Jan hurried to lead them to the stable. He took Eva from Charles's numb arms, then helped Charles dismount. Charles stumbled when he tried to walk. His knees felt weak, and he was exhausted.

Dawn began to break.

No sooner did Charles walk through the doorway than Mrs. Baumann bustled toward him. She had roused all the other servants and lit all the lights.

"Milord, we feared for your life, out in that storm!" she cried, still in a state of high agitation. "Hannah, Marie, take . . . *her* into the library. Milord, take off that wet coat before you catch your death." She drew his greatcoat off his shoulders. "There's a fire laid in the library. Hannah! Pour his lordship a brandy!" She hurried Charles toward the library, then glanced back at Jan. "And you, stop dripping mud onto the floor, get back to the stable and see to his lordship's horse."

In the library, Charles managed to shrug her off long enough to see to Eva. Hannah and Marie had dressed her in a warm flannel nightgown and wrapped her in a blanket. To his relief, she had revived. But for her shivering, and a far-away look in her storm-bright eyes, she appeared unharmed. Relieved, he sagged into his chair. He wanted nothing but peace and quiet and a dry pair of trousers. But he endured a half-hour of Mrs. Baumann's solicitude, he put on an entire change of clothing, and he drank two fingers of brandy before he regained enough strength to send her and the other servants back to their beds.

Finally only the crackling of the fire broke the quiet. Eva stared into the flames. She glanced at him, silently repeating the questions she had asked in the cemetery. His gaze touched hers, then broke away, and he stared into the amber brandy. His hands warmed the glass; the intoxicating fumes rose up around his face. Though he was half drunk, he could feel the tension increasing between them.

"When you were . . . found," Charles finally said, "and brought to me, you remembered nothing."

"I know," she said.

"But I gave you a name, and a place. I gave you back your life. I can't send you home, because I don't know where that is. But I can give you a life, *here* and *now*. If you trust me. *You must trust me.*"

She stared into the fire.

"Yes . . ." she said. "But I'm cold."

"Cold! With this fire and that blanket, and half a pint of brandy in you?"

"I'm cold," she said softly, as if the fact amazed and frightened her.

She was shivering. He started violently at the chill of her

hands, remembering— He pushed the thought from his mind. The scars on her wrists had faded nearly to invisibility.

He knelt on the rug beside her and took her in his arms. She huddled against him, and her shivering stopped. Soon she had fallen asleep.

Charles brushed a lock of Eva's damp hair from her cheek. Every time he looked at her, she was more beautiful, whether he saw her outdoors in the sunlight, reading by candlelight, or, as now, in repose with the firelight on her tawny skin. He wondered if she would remember tonight when she next woke, or if the events would fade into her memory, like her first few hours of life.

"Come, Eva. Time for bed."

He eased her to her feet and helped her upstairs as one would help a sleepy child, never completely waking her. He put her to bed and drew the covers up around her, then sat by her bed and watched her.

Her actions tonight disturbed him deeply. Could it be that she retained some knowledge, deep in her mind, of the truth of her existence? If she became aware of it, she would hate and fear him. She would flee from him. When Mrs. Baumann came to him crying that Eva had disappeared, he had had a horrible moment of believing Eva had discovered something of her real history, that she had taken her independence in her own hands, that she had left him. Losing her was one of the few things in the universe that Baron Charles Frankenstein feared.

She shifted and sighed. She was graceful even in sleep. Moonlight cut through the breaking storm clouds, casting a silvery light over her, as if she were underwater, as if she were Aphrodite waiting to be born, waiting to steal away the wits of men.

She could not know where she came from, he thought.

She has no way of finding out. I am the only being alive who knows what she must never discover. She must never leave me. She *will* never leave me.

Eva shifted again, and her eyelashes fluttered. A sudden and unreasoning terror engulfed Charles. He feared that if she woke and saw him looming over her, she would learn—something. He rose and backed away, out of the moonlight. Eva woke for a moment and sat straight up in her bed, staring into the darkness. But she saw nothing save the shadows of her dreams. Soon she cuddled down in her bed again, and once again she slept.

Charles stole from her room and returned to the library. Standing before the rippled silver mirror, he extended his hand and touched the cool surface; he gazed into the image of his own intense eyes.

The silvered glass slid aside.

Entering his secret room, he let the mirror shut him away from the world outside and in with his most esoteric books, his alchemical equipment, his mechanical inventions. Some of the books he owned, if they were known to the world, would cause his ruin.

After lighting a black wax candle, Charles settled down on a soft leather cushion. He filled his water pipe with opium.

He drew the soft pungent smoke deep into his lungs, and let it carry him into a fantastical reverie.

Chapter 7

Rinaldo viewed the city from his perch on Viktor's shoulder. He had a certain fear of crowds, at least of crowds close around him. But this was not half bad, not half bad at all. He rode far above people's knees, far above the crush. For once he could afford to ignore the pitiful state of public sanitation.

From eight feet above the ground, Budapest was a colorful pageant. Rinaldo felt as if he were leading the parade. He pretended to be oblivious to the people, the noise, the excitement, while Viktor gazed at each new sight with undisguised wonder.

Rinaldo was not unaware that he and Viktor presented an arresting sight. Though Viktor was no longer quite so frightening as when Rinaldo first met him—his ragged hair had grown out and his terrible scars had faded; and Rinaldo fancied that he was far more presentable in his mended, cleaned clothes—his size alone would have drawn the attention of the farmers and peasants selling their cabbages and beets.

Two soldiers, splendid in their imperial uniforms, came riding down the street, letting their horses shoulder a clear path. Rinaldo, with his trained sense for danger, began to search for alleyways and dark corners, any place of escape or concealment. But the soldiers eyed Viktor's massive nobility, cast questioning glances at each other, and rode onward, having wordlessly decided not to demonstrate their

The translucent linen concealed yet accentuated the new being's magnificent form. Charles beheld a cocoon, ready to free a butterfly such as the world had never seen.

"I give you the new bride of darkness! I give you—the new Eve!"

The creature gazed upon the new being, who stood stiff with terror, looking wildly for escape. The pleading expression on the creature's face changed gradually to comprehension, and finally to rage.

"She could not know where she came from," he thought. "She has no way of finding out. I am the only being alive who knows what she must never discover. She must never leave me. She *will* never leave me."

Hannah reverently picked up the necklace Frankenstein had asked Eva to wear—a family heirloom. "Miss Eva, you're a vision!" Hannah said.

The countess glanced casually at Eva. Eva knew that she had already been inspected, and possibly, judged, before she could fairly begin to play her part.

Josef stopped and took a deep breath. "I was just going to say that you seem...different...from other girls of your station."

Rinaldo found the giant a most interesting fellow, and possibly useful to boot. Around here anyone outside the limits of average was marked by evil, fair game for torment. But even a zealot would think twice before trying to torment a giant. Even a dwarf might be safe with such a traveling companion.

Tonight was their last performance for Magar's Circus. Rinaldo had warned Viktor not to tell anyone they were leaving. Viktor had kept the secret, though he did not see how anyone could stop them even if they wished to try.

Eva felt as if she embraced the whole universe, as if she held its beauty and power in her hands. The castle lay transformed around her, changed from a quiet, gloomy, outdated old house to a magic crystal palace.

"I sewed you together out of corpses, and brought you to life by means of an electrical charge. I created your body just as I created your mind....And I can uncreate it too."

"You always were afraid of fire, weren't you!" Frankenstein said. He jabbed at Viktor again. "Now you have cause to be afraid, sir."

"Then you must tell me," she said. "You must tell me everything! And I— I have so much to tell you. The world is so big. It's so full of things, all waiting for us to see them..."

power and authority on this fine day. Viktor lacked the experience to be afraid; he stared at them with the awe of a child.

Rinaldo surveyed the market critically. Viktor's pack contained bread and cheese and wine; what need had they of anything here? It was nothing compared to the marketplace in Paris. But suddenly he beheld a sight he had not seen in far too long.

"Let me down, Viktor!"

The giant stopped and bent down. Rinaldo leaped to the ground, fishing in his pocket for a copper. He scuttled between legs and around feet. He reached up over the edge of the vendor's tray and tapped the copper on it.

"Two, please," he said.

The vendor, barely glancing at him, perhaps thinking him a child, took his copper and handed over two candied apples. Rinaldo grabbed them and ducked back into the crowd, looking forward to Viktor's expression when first he tasted what Rinaldo brought to him.

He reached the spot where he had left the giant.

Viktor was gone.

First concerned, then worried, finally frantic, Rinaldo hurried from one side of the street to the other, finding no trace of his friend. Somewhere along the way he dropped the candy apples. But he no longer thought about candy apples. He thought about Viktor's pack, which contained everything Rinaldo owned; he thought about being able to ride on the giant's shoulders and see above the crowds as he never could before, he thought about not having to fear the jibes and blows of normal-sized people. . . .

And he thought about his friend, who could not survive in this world, with his innocence and inexperience.

Rinaldo turned suddenly and bumped into the highly polished boots of a gentleman, who stumbled over him, regained his balance, and cursed delicately.

"What's this? Beastly little man! Out of my way!"

He kicked Rinaldo in the side, watched with satisfaction as Rinaldo sprawled onto the cobblestones, and strode away without a second look.

Dizzy and aching, Rinaldo pushed himself painfully to his feet and continued his search for his gigantic friend.

I have never seen anything so wondrous as Budapest. Rinaldo described it as we traveled here, though he holds Paris and Berlin—and his fond fantasy of Venice—above it. But I do not remember anything like it. At first I was frightened. We passed through the city gates, where a dead man hung by his neck from the wall. I stopped, I stared, for the sight reminded me of things I would prefer never to remember. Rinaldo chided me for my fear, pointing out the sign hung around the poor wretch's neck: Murderer. As long as I do not kill anyone, Rinaldo said, I will not come to the same fate. I tried to reassure him, for I have no wish to hurt or kill anyone, even Frankenstein, but my voice failed me.

I also feared the city people, for they could attack us and throw us in another river or in some deep dungeon such as the one in which Frankenstein tried to hold me. But, though they watch me sidelong, their attention seems more curious than fearful. Could it be that here they see many more fearful sights? Could it be that Rinaldo has brought me to a place where I will not cause terror by my very appearance?

A moment ago Rinaldo demanded to be put down. I obeyed, for he has more knowledge than I of the city— indeed, of almost everything. But I have not seen him since, and I am worried. I allowed my attention to be distracted by the sights and sounds and smells, and now I cannot find my small friend. I raise up on tiptoe to look for him, but that does not give me much advantage that I do not already possess. Perhaps he has gone to one of the market stalls—but I cannot find him there, either.

Ahead lies an open square, a bit of meadow. Perhaps he felt lonely for forests and fields. Perhaps he is there.

The people make way for me. More stalls stand in the meadow. Ahead is a small pavilion with a curtain across its front. Many small people sit in front of it! But they are children. I cannot see Rinaldo. Perhaps I passed him in the street; perhaps he is still on his way here.

I sit down to wait.

Suddenly the curtain sweeps aside. A loud, high-pitched cheer erupts from the crowd. It startles me, but then I see what they are looking at.

It is amazing. I did not know that people existed who are smaller than Rinaldo, but two tiny people hardly bigger than my fist appear in the opening the curtain reveals. The tiny man is very ugly, and the tiny woman very beautiful, yet they dance and play with each other, and the tiny woman is not frightened. They are dressed in bright colors. They are wonderful!

But suddenly a third little person leaps out from the back of the pavilion. He must have been hiding there! He wears black, and—how strange!—he bears small curving red horns on his forehead.

The crowd around me gasps with fear. They cry to the small man, *Look out! Look out!* But he does not heed them. The horned man suddenly snatches the small woman from her dance. Now the small man sees him and notes what he has done. I wonder if I should try to help him. But suddenly he turns to the crowd and opens his arms, as if to say, Did you see that? *Did you see that?* Well! I must remedy *this* turn of events!

The small people around me laugh, and I laugh too.

Laughing does not hurt me as speaking does. It is wonderful!

Everyone hears me. They all look at me. Now they will scream with fear—

But they do not. They smile at me, they laugh with me, they point to the pavilion.

The horned man hits the small man, who falls somewhere out of sight. The horned man holds the small woman—he must be hurting her, for she is trying to escape. A child grabs my arm, frightened. Now I *must* do something.

But suddenly the small man appears again. He carries a club. He knocks the horned man down. The horned man releases the small woman. He flees. The small woman is saved!

I laugh with relief, and all the people around me laugh, too. The small, beautiful woman kisses the small, ugly man, and then they face the crowd and bow deeply. I do not quite understand what has happened, but it has all turned out for the best.

Rinaldo finally found Viktor sitting with a bunch of children, blithely watching a harlequinade, blithely unaware that his being lost had driven Rinaldo to distraction this past half hour.

"What are you doing?" Rinaldo demanded. He cuffed Viktor on the side of the head, his action fueled as much by concern as by an attempt to conceal his relief.

Viktor pointed to the puppet stage. "Men," he said. "Little men. Like you."

"I beg your pardon," Rinaldo said.

"And little woman," Viktor said, oblivious to Rinaldo's annoyance. "*He* steals her—*he* comes with a stick and hits and hits. She—"

"Splendid," Rinaldo said. "Magnificent. Brilliant drama. Can we go now?"

Viktor glanced at the stage again, a pleased smile on his face. He took no note whatever of Rinaldo's exasperated tone. Happily, he lifted Rinaldo up to his shoulder. His humor was so good that finally Rinaldo could not help but smile.

"Let's go," he said. "We've got work to do."

The circus was not what Rinaldo had hoped. He, who had performed for the crowned heads of Europe, working for a mere carnival—! It would be a step down in this world. But, Rinaldo reflected, sometimes one must take a step down in order to reach the next step up.

Viktor was as balky as a mule. Again and again he stopped to stare at sights upon which Rinaldo would not have wasted a second glance: a pair of jugglers who dropped their clubs at every other pass, who were not fit to shine the shoes of the famed Russian jugglers, Fyodor and Mikhail, with whom Rinaldo had traveled for a season. The main tent, magnificent to Viktor, threadbare and pitifully small in Rinaldo's more worldly experience. The animal pens, containing a mangy bear and a scurvy lion; a few scrawny horses; a sickly-looking elephant. Rinaldo remembered the magnificent beasts brought to entertain the court of Napoleon and Josephine: tigers and leopards, man-apes and monkeys; even a cheetah in a golden collar who would chase down a rabbit and drop it at its owner's feet.

But there was no point lamenting lost times.

Finally they made their way to the caravans on the other side of the compound. Outside the largest wagon, the one with the least-peeled paint, Rinaldo jumped down from Viktor's shoulder.

"Wait here a minute," he said.

Viktor nodded, only too happy to stay outside and watch.

Things were not going well.

Magar, the circus manager, listened emotionlessly. He never frowned in sympathy at the trials Rinaldo had gone through to get here; he never laughed at his jokes. What was more, his clothes were dirty and he had worn them several days too long; and apparently he had decided to stop shaving on the same day he decided not to change his clothes. Rinaldo had to work at it to like him.

"I am celebrated throughout Europe," Rinaldo said. "My partner and I—"

"The fact is," Magar said, "I don't need a midget."

Rinaldo's work went for nothing; the fact was, he could not make himself like Magar. But these were hard times, and one must make the best of the opportunities life presented.

"Not *a* midget, Mr. Magar," Rinaldo said indignantly. *"The* midget."

He drew a wallet of oiled silk from inside his coat. Neither rain nor river water had penetrated it; the document lay safe inside. He drew out the stiff paper, opened it, and smoothed the red ribbon sealed to it with scarlet wax.

"I have here," Rinaldo said, "a document signed by Wilhelm Kastor, renowned doctor and phrenologist of Krakow, stating that I am, beyond question, the smallest living human on the continent of Europe and in all the Russias."

Magar had already begun to look bored before Rinaldo mentioned the good doctor. The circus manager jerked open a drawer and flung a handful of parchment pages onto his desktop.

"I got papers that say the same thing from every midget that ever worked for me." Magar stood up and leaned forward, looming over Rinaldo. "What do you take me for? The fact is, I don't need a midget. The fact is, people are tired of midgets. And so am I. The fact is, *I* need somebody that can drive tent pegs."

Raising his eyebrow as Magar spoke, Rinaldo did not flinch from the manager's ill humor.

"Stay right where you are," he said.

He opened the door, thinking, if Viktor has wandered off again, I'll—

Viktor stood near the bear cage, gazing with awe at the decrepit animal.

"Viktor!"

Viktor ambled happily back to Rinaldo. The wooden floor quivered as he mounted the steps. Even the phlegmatic Mr. Magar showed some small evidence of startlement when Viktor, stooping, entered the caravan.

"Think he might do?" Rinaldo asked innocently.

Of no mind to take Rinaldo's word for anything, Magar led the pair across the compound. A tired work crew labored to pitch one of the smaller tents, slamming their mallets again and again against long stakes that had barely begun to penetrate the hard-packed earth.

"One of you give him a mallet," Magar said, indicating Viktor. "And stand back."

The pair he addressed gratefully left off working. Viktor took the mallet and looked at it curiously.

"Hit that stake with the hammer and knock it into the ground," Rinaldo said.

The two men from the crew glanced at each other, finding some amusement in the spectacle of a midget directing a giant; they obviously thought Viktor too stupid to follow the simplest of orders.

Viktor hefted the mallet, lifted it above his head, and let its head fall upon the end of the stake. The stake slid smoothly into the earth, leaving not a finger's width of its length above the ground.

Magar frowned. "Tell him not to drive 'em so deep," Magar said to Rinaldo, as if he assumed Viktor could not even hear for himself. "But he's got the job. On trial. Half wages. And I still don't need a midget."

Rinaldo grabbed his sleeve as he turned away.

"We sign on together or not at all."

Magar glowered at him.

"All right," he said. "You can share one wage between you."

"To start," Rinaldo said.

"Take it or leave it." Magar appeared near the end of what little patience he possessed.

"We," Rinaldo said with dignity, "will take it."

Magar glanced around the compound. "Bela!"

The man who answered his shout appeared to take his style of dress from his employer. He rose unhurriedly from the bundle of straw upon which he had been lounging, supervising the work crew, and sauntered toward them.

"Take the ape," Magar said, "and go set the rest of the stakes."

Rinaldo flinched at the insult to Viktor, but Viktor showed no evidence of distress. In fact, Bela looked far more uncomfortable than Viktor.

Quite possibly, Rinaldo thought, my friend does not even know what an ape is. Another gap in his education—which, for the time being, I judge it best not to repair.

Magar put his hands on his hips and looked down at Rinaldo. He gave an enormous, long-suffering sigh.

"And let's see what you can do," he said.

Rinaldo followed him into the main tent. All he needed was a chance to demonstrate his performance, and he and Viktor would have a place as long as they needed it.

The piny scent of sawdust brought back such memories—!

As Magar settled onto one of the rough wooden benches that encircled the single ring, Rinaldo took a turn around the tent. The torches were not yet lit, but the daylight was strong enough and the tent worn enough to admit sufficient light. The trapeze hung perhaps fifty feet above the ground —sufficient, if barely, to give the audience a thrill. The lack of a net would simply add to the suspense.

Rinaldo slid his hand along the guy wires. Rust spotted them here and there, but they retained an essential soundness.

He grasped the ladder, set his foot upon the first rung, and took a deep breath.

"Now, I do my act on the trapeze." He climbed quickly to the platform.

Magar yawned. "How exciting." He barely bothered to glance upward.

Rinaldo freed the bar, ignoring the touch of dizziness. It never troubled him once he had begun to perform. He climbed onto the bar and started swinging, balanced unsteadily.

"First I tell a few jokes about how scared I am."

"Ha, ha," Magar said heavily.

"Then I wobble a bit." He hooked the supporting rope in the crook of his arm and spun around, fetching back onto the bar. "I do a bit of business here." He pretended to slip and fall, but grabbed the bar on the way past. He swung back to his feet and balanced there.

"They love it," he said.

Magar rolled his eyes at the sky in supplication.

"Then I— Oh, my God!" he cried, and leaped into the air. On the way down, he grabbed for the trapeze. His fingers moved quickly.

He missed his grasp.

As he fell he heard Magar's inarticulate cry of shock and surprise.

Ten feet above the ground the harness tightened around Rinaldo's chest and shoulders, and the wire supporting him thrummed with tension. It reminded him how long it had taken him to perfect fastening it to the trapeze when he fell. One had to be subtle, or the trick was revealed.

He hung bouncing in midair.

Magar sat down again, pretending he had known all along what Rinaldo planned.

Rinaldo unfastened the hook from his harness and somersaulted the last ten feet to the sawdust, landing lightly and expertly, as if it had not been two years since last he performed on the trapeze.

"I hook it up top when I fall, and it feeds from a spool on the harness." He opened his coat and showed Magar the straps. He grinned. "It gets 'em on their feet, all right."

"I've seen it before," Magar said. "A hundred times. In Prague. But . . . that was years ago. And who the hell goes to Prague?" He considered. "It'll do."

"I should think it will," Rinaldo said.

"You and the ape can sleep in the properties van. If you can fit him into it."

"His *name* is Viktor."

"What do I care," Magar said with unfeigned indifference, "what his name is?"

Rinaldo made up his bunk with satin sheets and a fur coverlet, Viktor's with silk and heavy quilted brocade. If the silk and satin were the threadbare remains of a curtain, the fur the moth-eaten skin of a bear that had died in the service of Magar, and the brocade the cast-off trappings of a worn-out howdah, for now they would suffice. Soon Rinaldo would replace them with something better. Better bunks, a better wagon—a caravan of their own. Perhaps, not too far in the future, their own circus playing the capitals of Europe.

Viktor touched the spangles on his bedding and smiled with approval. He had spent most of the past half hour exploring the van, with its litter of props and gear and odds and ends. Rinaldo took a huge feathered turban from the wall and placed it rakishly on his head.

"We're in business now, my friend," Rinaldo said. "We're on our way. Fame and fortune lie ahead, troubles all behind."

Viktor lay down on his bunk and stared up at the ceiling, still with a foolish smile on his face.

"What are *you* thinking about?" Rinaldo asked.

"I want . . ." Viktor said in his cracked whisper, "to ride a horse."

"Do you, now?" Rinaldo spread his arms and laughed. "One day in the city, and he wants to be a gentleman!"

Chapter 8

Hannah arranged Eva's hair into a mass of ringlets, and dressed it with a fine strand of pearls. Eva submitted to her attentions. She would much have preferred to be riding. She looked forward to meeting other people, but the preparations were endless and tedious. The dressmaker had made Eva stand through hours of fittings. Yet the new scarlet gown bore very little relation to the shape of Eva's body, so beneath it she must wear strange bits of clothing that pushed and pinched her into the proper form. Hannah had tried to explain why this was necessary, but on certain subjects Hannah was a most unsatisfactory informant.

She was, however, an excellent lady's maid. No longer did her hands snag the satin of Eva's dresses, no longer did she come to Eva smelling of greasy pots, and no longer did she cringe at the sound of Mrs. Baumann's voice.

The housekeeper had spent an entire day alternating between apoplexy and complete nervous prostration, after Eva informed her with some satisfaction that Hannah was no longer the scullery maid.

Hannah put the finishing touches on Eva's hair and dabbed her throat with perfume.

"Miss Eva, you'll look more beautiful than ever tonight!"

Hannah helped her into the scarlet satin dress. Finally, reverently, she picked up the necklace Frankenstein had asked Eva to wear. The gold settings and the rubies clinked together with a sliding silken sound, as soft as the rustle of

Eva's gown. The jewels were heirlooms of Frankenstein's family.

The cold metal warmed to Eva's body. Hannah fastened the clasp of the necklace, put the earrings on Eva's ears, fastened a ruby bracelet around her wrist, and stood back to admire her.

"Miss Eva, you're a vision!" Hannah said.

"I feel absurd," she said. "These clothes are nonsensical."

"They will please the Baron," Hannah said.

"Then he is welcome to try to wear them," Eva said.

Hannah giggled, as if Eva had made a joke, but Eva was quite serious.

"All the other women will be jealous of you," Hannah said, "and no man will have eyes for anyone but you. Especially milord."

Eva started toward the door. Walking was difficult in the fancy gown and the heeled shoes she wore, but with care and a bit of attention, one could contrive a certain grace.

"Miss Eva, where are you going?"

"Downstairs," she said. "It is time to leave."

"You cannot go down yet!"

"Hannah, whyever not?"

"You'd be on time—no, Miss, you'd even be early! It's impossible!"

"I don't understand."

"A lady must always keep a gentleman waiting, a few minutes at least, or the gentleman will think she's too eager."

"Too eager for what?"

"To command his attentions."

"I have Frankenstein's attentions all day and half the night," Eva said. "I hardly need to command them."

"Oh, Miss, you mustn't say so!" Hannah began to blush.

"Very well," she said, giving up her attempt to understand Hannah's reasoning. "If it will please you, I will stay here until you tell me I have made Frankenstein wait long enough."

Hannah finally decided that Eva was sufficiently late. Eva paused at the top of the stairs, for she heard Frankenstein's angry voice echoing from the foyer.

"Late!" he said with asperity. "Late! I can't believe it!"

From the foot of the stairs, Mrs. Baumann replied, "It's very like a lady, ain't it, milord?"

"What?" Frankenstein said. Then, "Oh. Yes." His anger seemed to fade. "Yes, it is."

Hannah smiled at Eva, as if to say, Didn't I tell you?

Eva descended the stairs.

Frankenstein glanced up, frowning as if to scold her, as indeed Hannah had said he might. But the moment he saw Eva, his expression changed. He watched her as if he had never seen her before. When she reached him, he took her hand and bent to kiss it.

Even Mrs. Baumann appeared not entirely displeased.

Frankenstein looked into Eva's face.

In the time she had been here, he had been angry at her, he had been pleased with her, he had scolded her, praised her, and argued with her. She had never felt afraid of him, even the first few days when confusion made her frightened of almost everything. But this strange and unfamiliar expression, compounded of anger and pleasure, did frighten her.

Hannah arranged the cloak around Eva's shoulders, smiling happily. She obviously found Frankenstein's reaction appropriate.

"The carriage is waiting, Eva," Frankenstein said. "We mustn't be late."

"No," Eva said levelly. "We mustn't."

Frankenstein picked up a polished wooden box and carried it with them.

Eva had never ridden in a carriage before. It was, she thought, like a small parlor on wheels. Jan sat on top to handle the reins; Eva had to sit inside where she could barely see the landscape. Frankenstein closed the windows and fastened them.

"You don't want to get a chill," he said.

"I am not cold."

"The wind will disarrange your hair."

Hannah had fastened Eva's hair with so many pins that Eva doubted it would dare to become disarranged, but she recognized the tone in Frankenstein's voice that indicated nervousness and a disinclination to argue. Arguing with him could be frustrating, since more often than not he would end the discussion by discounting Eva's opinion entirely and declaring himself the winner.

As the coach rolled down the steep road toward the town, Frankenstein grew more and more nervous. He fidgeted; he toyed with his walking-stick; finally he chewed his manicured thumbnail into a ragged edge.

"I am looking forward to the afternoon," Eva said. "I will be pleased to meet your friends."

"Yes, yes," Frankenstein said impatiently. "But remember what I've told you. Remember your manners. Remember—"

He launched into the same lecture he had given her this noon, this morning, and last night. Eva nodded when his tone seemed to require some reaction; surreptitiously she watched the town close in around them. The carriage kept out most of the new smells, and the noise of its wheels on cobbled pavement drowned out most new noises, but Eva could see and hear and smell just enough to be fascinated. They traveled through a bustling, colorful street, where people waved things at each other and shouted, and Jan had to shout, as well, to open a path for the horses. Frankenstein barely noticed. He finished his lecture and touched the wooden box possessively.

They left the marketplace behind and entered an area of large houses and gardens. A few minutes later Jan pulled up before an enormous mansion and opened the carriage door. Frankenstein got out, carrying his box, and handed Eva down from the carriage. She felt his tension. With Eva on his right arm and the box in his left, he strode up the steps.

"Remember what I've told you!" he said. "Remember *everything!* And—be calm!"

"I will," Eva said mildly.

As they reached the door, it swung silently open. The butler, an imposing elderly man in powdered wig and old-fashioned breeches and coat, stood aside to let them in. Other servants took their cloaks and gloves. The opulent house contrasted violently with the more restrained style of Frankenstein's house: Oriental rugs covered the floors, an enormous crystal chandelier loomed overhead, and the wallpaper glowed with painted scenes of exotic birds and flowers.

The butler led Eva and Frankenstein into the parlor and announced them. Frankenstein's tension heightened even more.

Eva hesitated. More people than she had ever met in her life fell silent and gazed at her: perhaps twenty men and women, each dressed more finely than the next.

The gas jets softly illuminated the polished wood and gold brocades of the furniture. Knickknack shelves and occasional tables littered the walls and floor. One displayed tiny whimsical carvings in an Oriental style, another small porcelain cups and saucers of varying designs; and one, placed discreetly and tantalizingly in the corner, held an array of exquisitely carven figures of men and women, all naked, all in odd and sometimes awkward positions. Eva wondered what they represented.

Frankenstein drew her farther into the parlor.

He led Eva to a woman of a certain age who wore a low-cut sapphire gown. The countess had obviously been a great beauty in her youth. Handsome still, she retained the presence of someone who expects compliments and flattery, and receives them. She sat in a brocade wing chair near the fire. All the other people ranged about her in irregular concentric arcs, ready to respond to her wishes, appreciate her wit, or make themselves useful to her.

Frankenstein released Eva's hand from the death grip of the crook of his arm. Only Eva noticed how tightly he clenched his fingers around the corner of his box. Feigning composure, Frankenstein bent over the countess's hand and raised it to his lips.

"Countess," he said.

"You've been a stranger to us, Charles," the countess said with mock chastisement, "and I think it's very wicked."

"Absent, my dear Countess, but hardly a stranger. Delighting you is my ceaseless occupation."

He put the box on the table before her, opened it, and drew out a marvelous toy, a glass globe containing a circle of tiny people so perfect they looked almost real. Everyone gasped, then fell silent with awe when he turned the gold key and the figures began to move. Dancing and bowing, they circled and spun, and as they pivoted about each other, they exchanged with each other their heads and limbs and torsos. A king pirouetted upon the feet of a goose-girl; the goose-girl wore the head and coronet of the queen. When each figure had regained its original form, they all bowed a final time and ceased their movement.

The assembled lords and ladies applauded.

"So charming, Charles." The countess squeezed his hand. "And so brilliant . . . when it suits you."

Eva realized something Frankenstein had not told her: that he—and no doubt every other person in the room—was involved in a performance of sorts, very little different from any of the plays she had read.

How interesting, she thought, to create one's own script, and try to weave it into the script all the other individuals are spinning for themselves.

"May I present Eva, my ward," Charles said.

The countess glanced casually at Eva. Eva knew that she had already been inspected, perhaps even judged, before she could fairly begin to play her part. She curtsied.

"Ma'am."

"Delighted," the countess said, without a trace of emotion or expression, and returned her attention to Frankenstein. She patted the seat of the sofa near her chair. He sat, and motioned for Eva to join him.

Frankenstein paid his attentions to the countess. Eva surveyed the other people in the room. Only one did she know: Frankenstein's friend William Clerval, whom she had not seen since his and Frankenstein's argument. He caught Frankenstein's eye, arched one eyebrow, and smiled wryly.

"Tell us, my dear," the countess said to Eva, "how you came to the House of Frankenstein."

Eva took a deep breath and launched into the story Frankenstein had concocted, which he had made her rehearse till she was sick of it. He had tried to explain why they could not simply tell the truth, that she had been found wandering and amnesiac; but Eva had found his reasons complex in the extreme.

"The Baron is a distant relation of my family in Budapest. When my father died, he left my guardianship in the hands of the Baron—"

"And shall we have some tea?" The countess smiled brightly.

"Thank you, ma'am," Eva said, and let her story lapse.

Two maids wheeled in a cart that supported an enormous gold samovar, many cups and saucers, and trays of small pastries. They set a serving table before the countess, but the countess sat languidly back and addressed Eva again.

"Since you're so near, my dear, and I'm so useless at my age . . ." She paused barely long enough for her guests to object to her self-deprecation. "Won't you serve us?"

"Of course, madame," Eva said.

Frankenstein sat forward abruptly, as if to prevent her, and Eva noticed Clerval stifling a laugh. Ignoring them both, she picked up a delicate porcelain cup, tilted the samovar forward on its supports, filled the first cup, and handed the fragrant tea to the countess.

"Your ward is most gracious, Charles," the countess said, a hint of warmth toward Eva in her tone.

Eva poured another cup and handed it to Charles, who accepted it with feigned casualness.

"The Baron has told me," Eva said, "that if I wished to learn graciousness I must sit at your feet, ma'am—since you are the very soul of it."

She smiled at the countess.

Charles's cup rattled against its saucer. He lowered the cup quickly to his knee. Clerval's snicker halted abruptly.

The countess smiled at Eva.

"And so very well spoken, too," she said.

Charles Frankenstein forced himself to loosen his grip on his delicate porcelain cup, before he crushed it. Perhaps all would be well. He had schooled Eva mercilessly. He himself had been living on the edge of nervous prostration. Time and again he had decided to forgo attending the countess's salon; time and again he had changed his mind.

William Clerval's unexpected presence had nearly un-
nerved him. William, who knew that Eva could shriek like a
catamount and rip raw meat with her teeth, now glanced at
Charles, smiled, and held his silence. He thought he knew
the truth; but the secret he kept was as much a lie as the
story Charles had concocted for the countess.

"Count Maleva was just speaking, Charles," William
said, "before you joined us, of Shakespeare's Richard the
Third—"

"I'm sure I have no opinion on the subject," Charles said
shortly, forgetting his manners for a moment.

The room fell into an awkward silence. Frankenstein
glared at Clerval. Charles had little real interest in literature, and Clerval knew it. Having kept quiet about Eva, no
doubt he felt justified in taking other amusements at
Charles's expense.

The countess's husband, the ancient Count Maleva, made
an aggravated "humph!" Charles felt himself blushing. The
count's preoccupation with Shakespearean scholarship had
slipped Charles's mind. This was not terribly surprising, for
the count himself often did the same thing.

"I think," Eva said suddenly, "that Shakespeare's histories are on the whole less satisfying than his fantasies."

"What!" exclaimed Count Maleva.

"The histories have a musty air, left over from the sources
which so heavily influenced him. Shakespeare was happiest
when he was dreaming."

"Who *is* this girl?" The count appeared both startled by
the spectacle of a beautiful young woman stating her opinions on literature, and intrigued by those opinions. Despite
himself, Charles, too, felt slightly shocked.

Eva leaned toward the count, about to explain her theory,
but a young cavalry officer interrupted her even before she
could speak.

"I think *all* books have a musty air, and I find all talk of them . . . intensely alarming."

Everyone in the salon laughed, even the count, and the tension was broken.

"And this a man who was *not* alarmed to charge a square of lances at Waterloo," the countess said, smiling fondly at the young man.

Charles had been so long out of touch with society that he did not recognize the officer. His isolation was not so great, however, that he failed to notice the large number of ribbons and medals arrayed across the scarlet uniform; nor did he— or the countess—fail to notice the officer's making eyes at Eva.

To Charles's relief, Eva left the dangerous topic of literature.

"Those who make history needn't read about it, need they, sir?" she said to the officer.

The officer bowed, accepting her comment as a compliment.

The countess leaned toward Charles. "She'll break a few hearts before she's through, will she not?" she said behind her fan.

Though Charles smiled and nodded, as he was expected to, the thought startled him. It had not occurred to him before.

"You must tell me, sir," he said abruptly to the count, "if you have caught the poacher."

As the count launched into a tirade against the presumption of the lower classes, Charles finally felt he could relax. No doubt he should have explained to Eva when it was appropriate to argue, and when it was more fitting to retire from the field; but she appeared to have figured that out for herself. Now she was chatting with the officer and laughing softly at his jokes.

Charles leaned back, sipped his tea, and let his attention stray. A sleek Abyssinian cat strolled out from behind the countess's skirt, looking for admiration. The countess bent down to scratch the chin of her pride and joy.

Suddenly Eva's cup and saucer crashed to the floor in a splintering of china and a splash of scalding tea. She leaped to her feet with a terrified cry. The cat jumped backward, bristling, ears flat back and tail lashing, hissing in fright.

Frozen with horror, unable to react, Charles watched Eva staring at the cat. Her eyes were fixed and unblinking. They changed, *somehow* they changed: the irises turned an eerie, unearthly violet. Her arms moved mechanically, stiffly, as they had not since the night of her awakening. The room fell into a deathly hush. Even Clerval paled with shock.

Charles leaped to his feet. His cup, too, crashed to the polished floor.

"Eva!" Charles said.

She jerked her head up; she looked at him but he did not know if she saw him.

She screamed.

The countess fainted dead away.

Clerval hurried to Eva's side.

"Eva!" He touched her shoulder. She spun toward him, pushing him away. Charles stepped forward and enfolded her in his arms. Together the two men urged her toward the door. Charles glanced back.

"The excitement," he said. "My ward is not used to—to being out in society . . . to the illustrious company." He was babbling, but he could not stop himself. "She was raised very quietly. In a convent. A convent of sequestered nuns. Under a vow of silence—"

"For heaven's sake, Charles, shut up," Clerval whispered violently, and dragged him and Eva from the salon.

In the entrance hall of the mansion, servants clustered

around them. One of the maids brought spirits of ammonia. Charles waved it away.

"Leave us," he exclaimed. "Bring our cloaks. We need no help. Call our carriage! She is only overexcited."

William took the vial, opened it, and waved it beneath Charles's nose. Charles gasped and coughed and sneezed.

"Have you regained your senses?" William asked.

"Yes, yes," Charles said quickly, fending off William's attempt to wave the smelling salts beneath his nose again. He put one hand on either side of Eva's face and looked into her eyes. The pupils remained dilated, her vision unfocused.

"You're such a fool, Charles," William said. "Didn't you learn any of the lessons I taught you? What is this idiocy? Eva, your ward? You could have told them the truth; they would have been fascinated. A young woman, found wandering in a storm—? Why, it's almost as good as illegitimacy."

"Shut up, William!" Charles said in his turn.

"Then you would have found it easy to explain her sudden lapse. Now . . ." William shrugged. "Unless you are careful, you will ruin her. But you so seldom take my advice . . . no doubt you'll tell everyone another lie, and another." He sighed dramatically. "When, my dear friend, will you learn that a mysterious hint of impossible truth is far better than the most elaborate, plausible lie?"

Charles turned furiously on his oldest friend and grabbed him by his perfectly tied neck-cloth.

"If you say another word to me right now, William, I will surely strangle you!"

The impassive butler returned with the cloaks. Charles snatched them from him, bundled Eva up, and hurried her out the front door.

Eva huddled in the corner of the carriage, wrapped in her cloak and Charles's as well. The awful blankness had left her eyes, and her body had relaxed from its tetanic stiffness, but now she wept, and could not stop shivering.

"Are you mad?" Charles shouted again. His hands trembled violently; only his fury kept him from a swoon. He saw the destruction of all his plans.

Eva raised her head and dashed the tears from her cheeks with the back of her hand.

"I was frightened!" she cried angrily.

"Frightened! Of a cat?"

"You never told me about cats! I thought it was a tiny lion."

"A lion!" He shook his head in disbelief. "How in God's name can I explain it? I shall have to say you're lunatic! And why I brought you—"

He stopped berating her. William's ideas began to sink in. His friend was better versed in the ways of the world than he. And if he was right, all was not lost.

"Oh, listen to me," he said in a mild and self-deprecating tone. "I sound like a dowager aunt." He chuckled, then burst into laughter.

Eva's anger faded, but she did not share his humor.

"I wanted to be perfect," she said sadly.

"You were magnificent!" Charles said, remembering her spirit and forgetting his own discomfort. "Let them talk. It will only make you more interesting."

Chapter 9

Rinaldo has covered his face with white and red paint. I am distressed by the strange scarlet gash of his mouth, the ugly wig with which he covers his hair. But he explains that he paints himself to make people laugh, that he wants people to laugh and that they will laugh. I do not understand, for I have seen him grow enraged when people have laughed at him or at me. I will watch, and try to comprehend.

He paints his face before a peeling mirror in our fantastically appointed van, muttering softly. Tonight he will give his first performance, and he is pridefully outraged that he must appear while the members of the audience are still finding their seats.

He is nervous, and this realization startles me. I think of Rinaldo as practically imperturbable, but he is subject to the same fears as I.

He has not explained to me what exactly he will do in the ring. I am to be surprised with the others. He says I will laugh. But I cannot laugh at Rinaldo. I admire him too much. I could never stand up in front of all those people and make them laugh at me.

He completes his disguise and jumps to his feet, fairly glowing with excitement and nervous energy; he motions to me to follow and bounds down the steps.

Outside the main tent, we wait. Some of the riggers have dressed in striped robes to parade around the ring and play raucously on flutes and panpipes. Bela, Magar's helper, gave me a whistle and made me play it. But my hands are too large and too slow. I tried to finger the notes; I failed. Bela laughed heartily.

He planned for me to fail, so he could laugh at my expense.

I crushed the wooden flute between my fingers. Afterward I was sorry, for I had destroyed something that someone else could have used to produce beauty.

The bareback riders and their horses stand nearby, wearing tarnished spangles and bedraggled feathers. Waiting to perform, the dispirited horses bear fire in their eyes. One can forget for a moment that they are poorly fed, poorly kept, and overworked. Horses retain an essential nobility, no matter their circumstances. I long to ride one. I can imagine cutting through the wind like a bolt of lightning, as clearly as if I had experienced it.

"Viktor!"

Rinaldo shouted to his friend to come and watch, then ran into the ring for his first performance in Magar's Traveling Circus.

Daydreaming again! Rinaldo thought, more amused than irritated. Daydreaming about horses, while I set us on the path to fame and fortune!

He raced across the sawdust, did a handspring into the center of the ring, and swarmed up the ladder to the trapeze. He grabbed the rung, freed it, and clambered onto it. The sight and sound of the crowd, the smell of sawdust and musty canvas, brought back a flood of memories. He thought, This is no time for *you* to daydream, either.

The benches were barely halfway filled. Magar did not trust Rinaldo to hold the attention of the whole crowd, only to amuse them as they filed in. Rinaldo smiled under his makeup. His low status would soon change. This circus was about to get its headline act.

Below him, Viktor stood just inside the tent, watching him with an expression of complete wonder. Rinaldo would have waved, but it would break the mood of the performance. The delight on his friend's face pleased him, but Viktor must stay farther from the ring. He drew the attention of some of the audience.

Rinaldo let the trapeze's arc slow and come to a shaky stop, as he himself pretended to tremble with fright. When he confided to the audience that he had been tricked into the aerial act and that he truly had no idea what he was doing up here, he began to get their attention. Viktor began to look distressed.

"They told me," Rinaldo shouted, continuing his story, "that she finds aerialists attractive, but—whoops!" He teetered on the bar, fell—the audience gasped!—caught himself, and swung back up. Viktor came a few steps closer, shrugging off Bela's restraining hand.

"Shh!" Rinaldo exclaimed. "Don't tell her I fell—maybe she won't notice." Viktor was nearly beneath him now, and Rinaldo wished he had explained to the giant what he planned to do. He swayed on the trapeze to increase its arc. Viktor stumbled back and forth, trying futilely to keep up with it.

"Perhaps if I just stand here," Rinaldo said, "and swing for a bit— Oh, my God!"

He slipped and took the fall. The audience shouted; many people leapt to their feet in disbelief. The catch wire sang, spinning out from his harness. Below him, Viktor cried out in a low, horrified moan and rushed to try to catch him. A few feet above Viktor's head, the wire jerked Rinaldo to a stop. He hung bouncing and laughing just out of his friend's reach. Viktor stared at him in shock. The audience let out its collective breath in a sigh of relief.

With a sudden inspiration, Rinaldo unfastened the wire and tumbled into Viktor's arms. Viktor caught him and held him up as if to be certain he was all right.

As the crowd erupted into cheers, applause, and laughter, Rinaldo climbed onto Viktor's shoulder and perched there, waving and bowing, as Viktor carried him from the tent.

Viktor returned Rinaldo to the audience three times before the cheering subsided.

Immediately after the performance, Magar ordered Rinaldo and Viktor to his caravan. Rinaldo took his time. He did not intend to renegotiate with the circus owner while dressed as a clown. But finally, when he had taken off his makeup and changed his clothes, when he decided Magar had waited long enough, and when he had basked in his triumph, he and Viktor answered the summons.

Magar looked up from his desk as Rinaldo entered.

"You should have told me about the change in the act."

"A last-minute inspiration," Rinaldo said easily.

"Which you'll continue to use," Magar said.

"Of course Viktor *can* do it," Rinaldo replied. "But it's going to cost you something. Full wages."

"That's out of the question!"

"You ought to pay him double wages anyway. He's saving you the labor of three men."

"Go outside and take a walk. I prefer to settle with the ape on my own."

"If I go, Viktor goes," Rinaldo said. "That's the way it is with us."

"Let him talk for himself."

Viktor simply gestured toward Rinaldo.

"My friend." His voice was lower, hoarser, than usual.

Rinaldo felt a pang of guilt, for his "surprise" had caused Viktor to shout during the performance, and it had caused the giant great pain.

Magar pounded his fist on the desk, but Viktor nodded toward Rinaldo again. Rinaldo turned his most innocent smile upon their employer.

"All right! Full wages!" Magar shouted. "On trial!"

"It's a deal."

"I don't like you, Rinaldo," Magar said softly. "That's something to remember."

Rinaldo tipped an imaginary hat. He and Viktor left the caravan, Rinaldo whistling softly, Viktor smiling over his friend's pleasure.

Before the next performance, Rinaldo refined the act. When Viktor realized that he must go out in front of the crowd again, he reacted in fright. Rinaldo managed to convince him that no one would scream at the sight of him.

"What do you think of your costume?" Rinaldo asked, a trifle hesitantly. Many men, even seasoned performers, had little taste for comedy and no taste at all for the sort of costume Viktor was putting on right now. But it would be so perfect for the act!

Viktor simply nodded as he fumbled with a fastening. Rinaldo finished buttoning him up and patted his wig into place. Grinning, he scrambled into his own new costume.

A few minutes later an enormous woman with her equally enormous infant wandered hesitantly into the circus ring, for all the world as if they had become lost. Viktor, in cloak, wig, and bonnet, led Rinaldo, in long shirt and lace cap, along by the hand. Viktor turned his back on his baby for a moment, and Rinaldo retaliated against his mother by scrambling to the ladder and climbing to the trapeze.

Rinaldo preferred this act to the original. He could show

off to his heart's content, instead of having to pretend he had only dared the trapeze because of unrequited love. As Rinaldo played the crowd, Viktor ran back and forth beneath the swinging bar, waving his arms, pretending to tear his hair, and giving a creditable imitation of a fit of hysterics.

Rinaldo bounced on the bar like a babe in its crib, tottered, teetered, spun. The audience cheered him on, gasping at his audacity, laughing at his "mother" as she ran back and forth beneath him, never quite able to keep up with the arc of the trapeze.

The babe fell with a great shrieking howl. His mother could not hope to reach him! Gasping, the people rose as one.

When he swung and bounced just out of Viktor's reach, they cheered with surprise and relief. Rinaldo freed himself and tumbled into Viktor's outstretched hands. Viktor tucked him unceremoniously beneath one arm and carried him away, pretending to spank him as they left the ring. The crowd laughed with delight.

That evening, Rinaldo left Magar's caravan clutching four gold pieces, his and Viktor's wages. Magar had, of course, tried to fob him off with three.

Rinaldo started as a shadow moved toward him.

But it was not a robber—not quite, or at least not at this moment. Bela, Magar's assistant, stepped out of the darkness.

"Anybody can do that wire trick," he said nastily. "That's what Magar says. It isn't you who gets 'em on their feet. It's the ape. We don't need you. We don't like you, dwarf, and you better remember it."

Rinaldo found a careless smile somewhere in the recesses of his pride and terror.

"Where have I heard that before?" he said. "I just wonder where I've heard that before."

The circus traveled on; Rinaldo and Viktor won more acclaim with every performance.

Once a week, Rinaldo rewarded himself by taking his and Viktor's savings out of its hiding place and counting it. Viktor insisted that Rinaldo keep all the money; he would not take his share. Rinaldo kept it safe for him; for Viktor, with his otherworldly innocence, would give it away to anyone who asked. Rinaldo fantasied constantly about what to do with the money: a caravan of their own; a stake to keep them in style when they decided to quit this fleabitten excuse for a carnival and join a real circus; even their own circus, managed well, with the best acts in Europe and Asia. But first, before any of that, he would see Venice, the jeweled city in its setting of the sea.

But Viktor? What about Viktor? He performed his role, at first because Rinaldo asked him to, and then because he enjoyed performing. But he showed only disinterest in success.

Rinaldo pushed the gold pieces into a pile, plucked one up, and let the light gleam from it.

"It won't be long now, my friend. The songs of the gondoliers . . . the lady of your dreams." He tossed the coin to Viktor, who raised his hand but was too slow to catch it. The coin landed on the floor, ringing as only gold rings. Rinaldo grinned and retrieved the coin. "You can buy a lot of shiny, sparkly things with a coin like that."

Viktor shook his head sadly. "She was beautiful. Like stars."

" 'She walks in beauty like the night', eh? Eh? That's poetry, Viktor. Poetry."

"Hates me," Viktor whispered.

"None of that, now! None of that! You just follow your heart and you'll be fine. Follow your dream." He patted his heart. "It's the key to everything."

Eva leaned close over the gray mare's neck and let her gallop down the path through the bare trees. The day was cold and invigorating. Eva loved to ride alone. She did not have to worry about holding back so Frankenstein could keep up with her. To her great relief he had stopped objecting to her rides, and stopped insisting that he must come along. He did not much enjoy riding, despite his beautiful, well-bred horses.

Now that he no longer needed to oversee every minute of Eva's education, he seldom rose till after noon. Most days, he closeted himself in his library with the curtains pulled shut, making no distinction between day and night. Sometimes Eva came back from riding to find that he had locked the library door and would not come out for food or conversation or sleep, sometimes for two or three days at a time. She worried about him as he became more distant from her.

He accompanied her to salons and parties, but grudgingly, and more and more rarely. As soon as he had shown her the world outside, as soon as he had proof that she could hold her own in company, as soon as exaggerated stories about her mysterious background circulated wildly, he began to refuse most invitations and stay home most evenings. It was as if he had set up an experiment, and, having completed it, lost interest in it. When Eva told him she did not mind going alone, he said that was out of the question. (Mrs. Baumann was aghast.)

Once in a while they did go out, and with each excursion Eva realized more clearly that the freedom she had perceived was an illusion, a mirage in a desert of rules and expectations. She chafed against the restrictions, considered them, worried them around in her mind.

Only when she was riding on the gray mare, all alone, could she feel free.

A horse and rider stood among the trees ahead. Eva shifted her weight and the gray mare slowed to a canter. Her ears pricked forward as she, too, saw the other horse. Eva brought her to a trot, though the mare wanted to run. She was an Arabian, bred for speed and war.

As she approached, Eva recognized the rider: the young cavalry officer from the countess's salon. Eva wished the trail had remained deserted, but the officer had seen her; and he had done nothing to earn her incivility.

He urged his horse out onto the path.

"Miss," he said. "I should hardly presume to speak to you, since we haven't been introduced—"

"But I saw you at the countess's," Eva said.

"Yes, of course, but not formally introduced, only—"

"Oh, don't be ridiculous," Eva said. "Tell me your name."

"I am Josef Schildman."

"My name is Eva."

"Eva." He bowed stiffly. "I am delighted."

Taking her hand, he bent down to kiss it. Eva was seized with an urge to kiss his hand in return, but she refrained.

"I stopped because . . ." Josef hesitated. "I'm afraid I've gotten lost. I was looking for the old road to the pass, but I seem—"

"I wouldn't go there, if I were you," Eva said. "The road is blocked in many places by fallen stones, and the mountain is still sliding."

"But I'm told the view is very fine."

"It is. But you might be killed."

"Ah, well, then," Josef said, making a gesture of dismissal, "in that case I shall just have to go and risk my life, won't I? I don't know what else a life is for."

"If you are determined," Eva said, "then I shall be pleased to go with you, and show you the way."

"Splendid! That is—unless you mind riding hard. This stallion won't stay to a canter, for the life of him."

"We will ride as hard as you like," Eva said. She touched her legs to her mare's sides, and the horse sprang into a gallop. Josef, laughing, followed close behind.

The forest gave way to the stony path below the monastery. Eva slowed her horse. Josef came to a sliding stop beside her.

"Giving up so soon?" he asked.

"You said you wished to see the view," Eva said. She swept her hand in an arc, presenting the green valley and the endless ranges of mountains. She loved to ride up here, to imagine what lay in the blue-gray distance, to dream of all the things she had read about but never seen.

"It *is* beautiful," Josef said, but his voice was so strange that Eva glanced at him.

He was not looking at the view; he was staring at her. He held her gaze only a moment before turning away to regard the scenery.

"Come a little farther," Eva said.

She turned her mare down a disused, narrow trail. An outcropping of stone bounded it on one side, and a sheer cliff fell away equally abruptly on the other. The mare danced along its edge. Stones clattered from her hooves and fell three hundred feet into the valley. Eva glanced back; Josef stared into the abyss. He looked up, saw her, and spurred his horse forward.

Farther on, the view was even more impressive for being wilder. Across the entire vista, not a single thing had ever been touched by man.

"Spectacular," Josef said. "Brilliant."

"It's lovely here," Eva said.

"And the danger adds its own particular spice."

"Yes." She supposed Josef was right, that the trail was perilous, but she had never thought of it before. "I like spices."

"Forgive me for saying this . . ."

Josef's voice sounded strange again. He turned away without meeting Eva's gaze.

"Please stop apologizing for everything," Eva said.

"Yes, certainly, I'm sor—" He stopped and took a deep breath. "I was just going to say that you seem . . . different . . . from other girls of your station."

Eva gave him a sharp look. "How am I different?"

"Most of the girls I know—those of your station, I mean —are a bit more . . . timid."

"Timid," Eva said. "Isn't that what the world wants women to be? And by the world, I mean men, who control it."

Josef laughed, avoiding any possibility of a serious conversation.

"I can see you're going to make some fellow a most disputatious wife."

"I hardly think *I* will ever marry," Eva said. "Marriage was created by men to keep women . . . timid."

"Oh, my," Josef said, sounding rather shocked. "But . . . I wonder if your guardian, the Baron, shares your advanced philosophy on the subject?"

"Of course he does," Eva said.

"I'm damned!" Josef exclaimed. He cut his words off, about to apologize again, but stopped in time. "I heard they bounced your baron out of university for his 'indecent ideas.' I'm glad to see the experience hasn't cowed him."

"The Baron is a great man!" Eva's intensity surprised her. "He isn't afraid of anything!"

"And so . . ." Josef said, "I suppose you will swear off love and romance."

"No."

Again he would not meet her eyes.

"I will do what I please," she said.

"Will you?"

She turned the mare and galloped down the precarious pathway, leaving Josef Schildman behind.

Rinaldo sauntered around the main tent, heading for the van.

"Look out, men! The ape's going to give us a demonstration of horsemanship!" Bela's laugh rose above the catcalls of the riggers clustered around the horse pen.

Viktor! Rinaldo thought. Viktor, daydreaming again! And daydreaming aloud, in front of Bela! What is innocence, in the face of malice?

He shouted, he ran, but he was too late. A frightened horse whinnied and bucked, its hooves scuffling and thudding in the dirt. It pitched Viktor to the ground with a tremendous crash.

He pushed between the legs of the riggers. Viktor lay senseless. The horse galloped frantically around the corral. Bela laughed wildly.

In a fury, Rinaldo launched himself at Bela's knees. The shock and surprise sent Bela staggering. Rinaldo wrapped his arms around Bela's leg and sank his teeth into his thigh. Bela shrieked like an animal and kicked frantically. Rinaldo clenched his jaws. The material of Bela's pants tore, then the flesh beneath. Bela screamed again. He smashed Rinaldo against one of the fence posts. The wind knocked out of him, Rinaldo lost his grip. Bela kicked again and sent him rolling through the dust and manure, till he fetched up gasping against the other side of the pen. He staggered to his feet, gagging on the salty taste of Bela's blood.

Bela pulled a knife from his belt and strode across the compound, limping and cursing.

Rinaldo spat on the ground and scrubbed his sleeve across his mouth.

"I heard you can get rabies from biting mad dogs," he said. He dodged; the tip of Bela's knife barely scraped the back of his coat. He scrambled for safety, but one of the roustabouts stuck his foot in the way and tripped him. He fell hard. Gasping for breath, he rolled painfully away from the next attack.

Viktor loomed head and shoulders over Bela. Bela felt his presence or saw his shadow. He spun straight into the face of Viktor's anger. Bela ducked beneath Viktor's arm and fled.

Viktor picked Rinaldo up, gazing at him as if to ask, Are you all right? Are you hurt?

Suddenly the horse neighed and snorted again. Viktor started violently. The roustabouts laughed. Still carrying Rinaldo, Viktor lumbered away in terror.

The door to their van slammed shut behind them; only then did Viktor begin to calm from his fright. He put Rinaldo on his bunk and stared worriedly down at him.

"I'm all right," Rinaldo said. "As long as that brute didn't poison me with his blood." He took off his coat to dust it. Bela's knife had slashed its shoulder. "There's another debt he owes me! My best coat!" He flung it aside and shook his head at Viktor. "My dear friend," he said, "how could you trust yourself in Bela's hands?"

Viktor sat in his usual spot, hunching even farther into the corner than usual.

"He say . . . ride." Viktor stared at the floor. "But . . . horse hate me, too."

"That particular horse hates everybody," Rinaldo said. "Haven't you seen how it flattens its ears and bares its teeth whenever anyone comes near? As well anyone might, horse or man, who was driven by Bela. Viktor, you cannot simply plunge onto a horse's back and expect it to obey you. You must pet it first, and talk to it. Let it know that you are not so fearful as you seem. Whisper in its ear." He suddenly grinned, unable to resist a joke. "That works with ladies, too, my friend."

Eva wandered through the castle, bored and lonely. Frankenstein was shut up in the library again. Everyone in the household knew better than to disturb him when he did that. Eva worried about him, he looked so pale and intense, but he only grew angry when she asked after his well-being.

The servants had their half-day off. Hannah had gone to town to visit her mother, so Eva had no one to talk to. She was tired of studying. All the books she had not read were locked up in the library with Frankenstein. The castle smelled strange. She had ridden all morning and now she was even tired of riding. She kept remembering the expression on Josef's face when he looked at her. She wished Frankenstein would look at her like that, but he never did, and she knew if she asked him why he did not, he would become cold and distant and tell her he could not yet answer her question.

She decided to explore parts of the castle that she had never visited. The view from the far tower must be excellent, but no one had ever showed her the way there, nor had anyone ever mentioned being in it. She turned down a corridor that led in the right direction.

She rounded a corner and came to a dead end. She

frowned curiously. This spot must be nearly within the tower, but she found no sign of a staircase or a doorway. Though other disused parts of the castle smelled damp and musty, here the smell of fresh mortar and new stone filled the air. Eva inspected the walls more closely and found the doorway that had been blocked up. The mortar gave slightly. The door had been sealed quite recently.

After a last look around, she continued her explorations elsewhere. But though she found some interesting nooks and crannies—even a dungeon!—she could not put the walled-off tower from her mind; nor could she find any other way, inside or outside the castle, to enter it.

That evening just before dinner, Frankenstein reappeared. He had on the same clothes he had worn the day before, his hair was uncombed, and his cheeks were covered with the fine blond stubble of his beard. Eva reached out to touch his face. He started and drew back sharply. She let her hand fall to her side, feeling confused. She did not understand why she had wanted to stroke his unshaven beard, even less why she had so powerful a tactile memory of what it would feel like. She had no memory of actually having done such a thing before.

During dinner, Eva tried to make conversation. Frankenstein, distracted, replied in monosyllables. He asked nothing of what she had learned or seen or done today.

"Why is the door to the tower sealed off?" Eva asked suddenly.

Frankenstein glanced up sharply, then recovered his composure. "There was a fire," he said coolly. "Part of the wall was destroyed. It isn't safe."

"Why have you never repaired it?"

"I have no need of the tower," he said, and went back to his dinner.

Eva ate another bite of roast beef—it was still too dry, too well-done, for her taste, but Mrs. Baumann had taken such offense at "interference" that Eva had never made another suggestion. She wished it were red and juicy inside, barely warm, nearly raw— Her mouth watered suddenly, surprisingly, and though she was half done with her meal, her stomach clenched with a desperate hunger. She put down her fork.

"Why were you dismissed from university?" she said.

"Who told you I was?"

"Josef Schildman—the countess's young officer. I met him riding in the woods. He was lost."

"Lost?" Frankenstein said. "That hardly seems likely."

He prodded a boiled potato with his fork, tried to pretend Eva was not waiting for a reply, tried to stare her down, and failed.

"I was dismissed," he said, "if you must know, for asking questions. They weren't the sort of questions professors want to hear. Questions about the limits of knowledge. The limits of science." He returned to his dinner.

Those seemed to Eva perfectly honorable and sensible questions, not at all "indecent," as Josef had referred to them. But many people misunderstood Frankenstein; she did not blame Schildman for envying her guardian's intelligence and accomplishments.

"Who found me in the forest near Brucor?" Eva asked suddenly.

Frankenstein's fingers tightened on his wineglass. He set it down very carefully.

"A . . . a woodcutter," he said. "You were unconscious. He took you to the doctor in the village, and he sent for me."

"And no one in the village recognized me?"

"No. Apparently you had . . . traveled a great distance." He touched her hand. "We made inquiries as far as Budapest. We received . . . no response."

"How strange," Eva said. No one missed me, she thought, no one looked for me. I might be anyone. Anything.

"Yes," Frankenstein said. "Yes, it is strange. You are a mystery, my dear. A genuine enigma."

He smiled. But Eva did not feel comforted.

Chapter 10

Outside the main tent, the noise of the crowd sounded muffled and distant, yet it told Viktor what act was performing and how it was being received as clearly as if he were watching it himself. Often he did watch. He still liked to see the horses, despite his unfortunate attempt at riding one.

Rinaldo was right, Viktor thought. I terrified the beast with my size and awkward eagerness. I cannot blame Bela for making jokes at my expense. Rinaldo and I, people like us, can only exist if we turn those jokes to our advantage. Rinaldo knows it, and he knows how, but I am still learning.

Tonight was their last performance for Magar's circus. Rinaldo had warned Viktor not to tell anyone they were leaving. Viktor had kept the secret, though he did not see how anyone could stop them even if they wished to try.

Rinaldo said Magar's troupe was insufficient to display their talents. He wanted to move on to a larger, finer circus. Viktor would have been content to stay, but he knew why Rinaldo truly wanted to go. Magar traveled nowhere near Venice. So Viktor accepted that they would leave. He was content to follow Rinaldo's dream.

Rinaldo and Viktor did not perform for some time yet, but Viktor did not like to be late. He returned to their caravan. Over time, its exotic contents had become familiar, even comforting.

The door hung open. Rinaldo must be getting ready early tonight. Usually, he found a good spot from which to watch the crowd. He claimed to Viktor that he counted the people, so Magar could not cheat them on their share of the money. But Viktor believed Rinaldo watched the crowd for the same reason he performed: because he liked to see people happy.

To Viktor's surprise, he enjoyed performing, and for the same reason. Sometimes he thought: Perhaps *she* will come to the circus. Perhaps *she* will see me, and laugh instead of screaming.

He entered the glittery dimness of the caravan. A dark shape beside his bed leapt around to face him. It was not Rinaldo—it was much too tall for Rinaldo. He stopped, confused.

Bela paled at the sight of Viktor, who wanted only to tell him not to be afraid. He would not harm him. He had not been angry with him because of the horse—only because he tried to hurt Rinaldo. Viktor wished Bela would promise not to lose his temper or try to hurt Rinaldo again. If he would, then perhaps Bela and Viktor could be friends.

But it was impossible. Those were too many words for Viktor to speak all at once, and Bela would not listen for as long as it would take him to say them.

"Where have *you* been? Where's Rinaldo?" Bela said sharply, trying to mask his fear with anger. "Magar's furi-ous—he needs you to go on now. The elephant's sick!"

"Rinaldo—"

Viktor tried to tell him where Rinaldo went to watch the show, but Bela was too impatient.

"Never mind!" he said. "I'll find him." Staying as far from Viktor as he possibly could in the cramped caravan, he hurried out.

How kind of him to find us, Viktor thought, How kind of him to try to deflect Magar's anger.

As Viktor prepared for their performance, Rinaldo ran up the stairs and into the caravan.

"Bela," Viktor said, "Bela—"

"I know!" Rinaldo said. "He told me." He ran past Viktor, grabbed up his costume from Viktor's bed, and ran back to the door, fastening his harness as he went. He paused only long enough to glance at Viktor. "Get moving, then! We're on!"

Viktor followed, putting on his costume as he went.

At the tent, Bela stood watching Rinaldo.

Bela's face wore an expression Viktor had never seen before. It held great satisfaction, yet great cruelty as well. Viktor stopped. He had never seen any sight so frightening.

Bela saw him. His expression changed to one of complete fear, from terrifying to terrified. Without a word, he fled.

And Viktor thought: Bela was standing near my bed when I entered the caravan.

Viktor thought: Rinaldo found his costume and his catch harness on my bed.

Rinaldo never left his costume out; he always checked the harness and the wire carefully, put it away, and got it out and checked it even more carefully before he put it on. Even if he did leave it out, why should he put it on Viktor's bed?

Viktor suddenly shivered. He felt that something was wrong, but he did not know what it was. He hurried toward Rinaldo to tell him what had happened.

"Rinaldo, Bela—"

A great burst of applause drowned out his words, and the bareback riders galloped from the tent. Viktor lurched backward to keep from being bowled over.

The audience gave another enormous cheer. As Viktor tried to reach his partner again, Rinaldo grinned and his lips moved in an announcement that Viktor could not hear, but knew by heart.

"That's us!" Rinaldo exclaimed.

Viktor tried to reach him, tried to call to him, but Rinaldo could not hear Viktor over the cacophony any more than Viktor could hear him. Rinaldo glanced at Viktor with a fond smile. His lips moved again; again Viktor could not hear him but knew what he was saying.

"What a team!"

"Rinaldo!" Viktor cried. He felt he must speak to his friend before they went inside the tent.

Viktor struggled to reach him, but Rinaldo ran into the ring just out of reach: it was all part of the act. He must stay ahead of Viktor, so even when Viktor ran faster, Rinaldo scampered out of reach, to the ladder, and up toward the trapeze. Viktor called out to him again, but the noise of the audience was deafening. Viktor grabbed the ladder and tried to climb up after him, but the rungs broke beneath his feet. The audience laughed hysterically.

Rinaldo cavorted on the trapeze. His joy in the performance radiated from him like sunlight. Viktor ran back and forth beneath him, trying to keep up with the arc of his swing, waving at him, crying out to him, trying to warn him not to fall. Viktor was afraid.

Rinaldo thought Viktor had added more antics to his part of the act. He waved down at his friend, pretending to be a spoiled child teasing its mother, but pleased by Viktor's animation.

Rinaldo slipped from the trapeze, caught himself, and clambered back to the bar. Viktor cried out again, but his words disappeared in the crowd's gasp of fear. Rinaldo laughed. He made the trapeze swing higher and higher. Viktor could not keep up with him.

Rinaldo fell.

Viktor heard the high whine of the harness wire spinning

out from its spool. He stumbled forward, trying to reach the spot where Rinaldo would fall.

He heard the high discordant note as the wire parted.

The ruffled edge of Rinaldo's gown brushed Viktor's fingers as he reached desperately to catch him. But he was too slow, too clumsy.

Rinaldo crashed to the ground.

The audience grew silent.

Rinaldo lay at Viktor's feet. He was very still. Viktor knelt beside him, but he did not know what to do.

Rinaldo opened his eyes. His right hand moved in a strange and awkward way. Rinaldo gasped at the pain of broken bones. With his left hand he grasped the safety wire and pulled it toward him.

Blood flowed from his nose, from his mouth. He lifted the end of the wire as if it were a heavy weight. He looked at its crimped, newly shiny end.

"Cut . . ." he said. He clenched his fingers around the wire. "Viktor . . ." he whispered, "carry me out of here. Quick. We'll . . . wreck the show."

His eyes closed. Viktor picked him up. He had carried Rinaldo halfway across Europe, but the walk across the ring seemed longer. Rinaldo was curiously light in his arms.

A few members of the audience clapped. Viktor did not acknowledge them. The animal trainer drove the dancing bear into the ring, and soon the audience was laughing and cheering again.

Rinaldo made a quiet sound. He was in pain, and the pain intensified when he moved. Viktor laid him down as gently as he could. Rinaldo still clutched the wire. He raised it and stared at it again, as if it could tell him the answer to some secret question.

Viktor knew the answer.

"Bela," he whispered.

Understanding entered Rinaldo's eyes, and, for the first time, fear.

"Get out of here, Viktor!" he said. "Take this. . . ."

He dropped the wire and fumbled inside his costume. He handed Viktor a chain and medallion. Viktor shoved it into his pocket. He would keep it for Rinaldo if that was what his partner wanted. But Viktor wished Rinaldo would tell him what to do. Why did he not tell Viktor how to make his nose and mouth stop bleeding? Rinaldo had always known what to do before.

"Take the gold," Rinaldo said. "And get out of here. Go find your lady."

"Rinaldo?" Viktor did not understand. They were going to Venice.

Pink foam covered Rinaldo's lips. A horse ridden near to death would bleed like that.

"Just follow your heart," Rinaldo said, "and you'll be fine."

"I have no heart," Viktor whispered. That was the closest he had ever come to telling Rinaldo all his truth, but he would make up for that, somehow. . . .

He knew it was too late.

Rinaldo raised himself up and reached out to Viktor; he touched the center of Viktor's chest, where he had seen an awful scar.

"Of course you have a heart," he said. "Because it's breaking."

His hand fell, and he collapsed. He trembled as if it were cold, but the day was not cold. His eyelids moved, and he looked at the sky. But he no longer saw Viktor.

"I guess Venice is out," he said. His whisper trailed off into silence. His eyes closed again. Something changed—it was as if he were there one moment, and gone the next.

One of the riggers pushed past Viktor, carrying a blanket.

Viktor wondered if perhaps Rinaldo were simply in some strange sleep. The blanket would keep him warm. But the rigger covered Rinaldo's face with the blanket.

Viktor reached to move the blanket. "No," he said.

Someone stopped his hand.

"No, stay back. He's dead."

"No!"

He struggled forward. Two of the riggers held him away.

"Yes, he is. Get back. Get away."

He could not understand what had happened, how everything could have changed so quickly. All he knew was that Rinaldo was gone, and that Rinaldo had told him to take the gold and leave. Perhaps if he did what Rinaldo said, everything would be all right.

He stumbled through the darkness to the caravan, his only thought to do as Rinaldo told him.

The door to the properties van gaped open again. The wavery light of a single candle spread across the steps, casting the shadow of an angry man. From the van came the sounds of tearing fabric and breaking boards. Frightened and confused, Viktor stopped.

"Where is it, you little runt?" Bela's voice matched his actions, tearing furiously through the night. "Where is it!"

He stamped down the stairs and across the compound toward Magar's caravan. Viktor moved hesitantly forward, slowly realizing and coming to accept the depths of hatred and greed to which Bela had fallen. He climbed the steps. All the sparkling finery that Rinaldo had arranged with such good humor lay torn and ruined in tangles on the floor. Viktor's vision blurred again. He blinked furiously. Tears ran down his cheeks. But in the midst of his grief, a terrible fury began to grow.

He reached into the trunk and removed the false bottom Rinaldo had built for it. He drew out the sack of gold coins,

the means to Rinaldo's dream. Now the dream felt empty
and hollow, like Rinaldo's body once the motivating spirit
of his life left it. Viktor put the sack into his coat and left the
caravan for the last time.

He crossed the compound, following Bela. His fingers
clenched into fists. The light of a lantern glowed against a
small window in Magar's caravan. Viktor looked inside.
Magar stared at Bela, his face pale, his expression horrified,
his voice shaky with shock and fear.

"I said I didn't like the dwarf." He shook his head at
Bela, as if his denial could change what had happened. "I
said I wanted him out of the way. I never said—"

Viktor moaned softly with grief.

"I know what you said, and I know what you wanted!"
Bela shouted. He grabbed Magar's collar and shook him.
"And you got it! So shut up!"

"I never told you to cut the wire. I never told you to—it's
like . . . it's like . . ."

Viktor cried out. His rage possessed him. He rammed
himself against the side of the caravan. The van shuddered
beneath the awful power of the giant. It tipped, then slowly
toppled sideways and fell with a crash. Inside, Bela and
Magar screamed. The lantern toppled, nearly died, and
caught its own spilled oil on fire. The light from the window
dimmed, then intensified.

The side door, now at the top of the fallen van, slammed
open. Bela scrambled out, flames licking at his heels. He
leaped to the ground. Viktor walked toward him, slowly as
always, but with the irresistible power of a natural force, a
moving glacier. Bela saw his movement from the corner of
his eye, spun toward him, and drew his knife.

The blade meant nothing to Viktor. His body and his
spirit carried the scars of wounds far worse than any Bela's
knife could inflict. His fingers closed around Bela's body.

Bela struggled and screamed. Viktor grabbed him by the throat to silence his screams. Bela dropped his knife. Viktor raised him from the ground, lifted him high over his head, and flung him violently across the compound. He crashed into the side of the lion's cage with a force great enough to rip the iron bars from the splintery wood that held them. Viktor crossed the compound. Oblivious to the snarling, growling lion, he reached into the cage, scattered the loosened bars, and dragged Bela up.

Bela did not scream, he did not move. His head flopped gracelessly sideways. His eyes were dull, and his tongue protruded.

Viktor understood death now. But he understood, too, that death came by different methods. Rinaldo had died slowly and in great pain. Bela died quickly. Viktor wished he had been more careful. He wished he had taken Bela to the top of the circus tent and dropped him precisely from a great height, so he too would have died with the pain of all his bones broken, with the pain of blood leaking from his veins and filling his body and his lungs, with the terror of being unable to breathe.

He let Bela's limp body fall. He had his revenge. But it meant nothing. His grief crept up and captured him again.

"Murder!"

Viktor turned and saw Magar staring at him from atop the toppled caravan.

"Murder!" Magar cried. He leaped from the burning wreck and disappeared into the night, screaming murder, screaming for help.

Slinking to the front of its cage, the lion peered into the night. Its eyes glowed like orange jewels. It stopped in the opening where the bars lay awry. The people who had hunted and caged it had trained and beaten it out of its need for freedom. And now they gathered, shouting and lighting torches as Magar urged them to hysteria with his cries of murder and betrayal. They gathered to hunt Viktor down.

He vanished into the darkness.

Hannah combed Eva's hair and arranged it prettily, but she knew nothing more to do for her tear-reddened eyes. Last night Eva had been seized with a fit of crying that she could not or would not explain. It had lasted for hours, and Eva, who usually hated inactivity, had kept to her bed most of the day. Hannah had her suspicions about why her mistress might be so upset—they were age-old reasons, but none the less painful for that.

"Miss Eva, do you want to talk about what hurts you so? Is it milord? Is he treating you badly? You know I'd not run and tell your secrets to others."

Eva took Hannah's hand and clasped it between hers.

"I know you wouldn't, dearest Hannah. But I truly don't know why I cried so last night. It must have been the dream. I had blood on my hands, yet I felt such grief, and I felt so defenseless—my life and purpose had ended." She tried to smile, though in fact an inexplicable depression still gripped her. She felt as if she had been betrayed and wounded. "I'm quite all right."

"You should rest," Hannah said.

"Charles will be upset if I do not join him to greet Mr. Clerval. And I wouldn't like to miss a visitor—we have so few."

"Hmmph," Hannah said. "I should think you'd take advantage of an excuse to miss this visitor."

"I know you don't approve of him. But he's very intelligent and entertaining."

"Excuse me, Miss. I spoke out of turn."

"No, you spoke your mind. We needn't always agree."

Eva went downstairs to join Frankenstein, leaving

Hannah to ponder the odd ideas of her mistress, who thought the minds of women equal to those of men, and the opinions of servants as worthy of consideration as those of masters.

Clerval arrived at Castle Frankenstein accompanied by a flurry of snowflakes and a positive storm of news and gossip from town. He greeted Charles as if the breach in their friendship had never occurred. He enlivened dinner with his tales of the count and countess, the last hunt of the season, and the visit of the infamous Lord Byron, whom Eva would have liked to meet.

They took their coffee in the library. Warming himself at the hearth, William took down the sword that hung over the mantel. He polished the dusty blade with his handkerchief.

"You should take better care of your trusty weapon, Charles," he said. "It served you so well, after all."

"You told me you never fought with it!" Eva said.

"And so I did not," Charles replied. "Not seriously."

"You give yourself too little credit, my friend. Eva, Charles was sabre-fencing champion at university one year —He never told you?"

"He never said a word about it."

"Well, he was. When I pointed out to him that a gentleman must be able to defend himself, in this world of brigands and robbers and offenses to one's honor, he took up fencing. And you must know Charles never takes anything up unless he has resolved to be eminently successful at it."

"It sounds exciting," Eva said. "Charles, will you teach me?"

"No," he said shortly.

He had never refused a request of hers so bluntly, even when she asked about subjects he believed she was not yet ready to learn.

Startled, Eva said, "But why not?"

"I've given it up. It's frivolous. There's too much strife in the world as it is. I'm done with sabre fighting."

Clerval chuckled. "He'd change his tune if he met a band of robbers in a dark alley."

Charles scowled. "Unlike you, Clerval, I don't frequent dark alleys."

"Nevertheless, every man should be able to defend himself," Clerval said.

"So should every woman," said Eva.

Clerval laughed, leaned over, and patted her cheek. "I'm sure there will always be a gentleman around to defend you, Eva."

"Put the sabre away, William," Charles said in a voice all the more discomforting for its utter tonelessness.

Clerval returned the sabre to its place, poured Charles a brandy, and changed the subject completely.

Eva sat by the fire, pretending to sew, wondering why Charles had reacted so strangely. From there her thoughts strayed back to her discomforting dream. When once more she paid attention to the conversation, it had turned to modern poetry.

" 'Forms more real than living man,' " Charles said, quoting. " 'Nurslings of immortality!' As I said, Keats's *Prometheus* is a case—"

"Shelley's *Prometheus,*" Eva said. She shivered suddenly. Those lines always made her shiver.

"It's Keats's, my dear," Charles said in a condescending tone. "If you don't mind."

"John Keats never wrote—"

"Will you kindly not interrupt me with this nonsense!"

His anger startled her. She had meant only to join in the conversation, which was, after all, why she supposed she was here. But now he glared at her with a certain sneer. Her own anger flared. Flinging her embroidery to the floor, she strode from the room.

William Clerval felt some satisfaction as Eva stormed out. He had warned Charles of the consequences inherent in his plans for Eva's education.

"The trouble with free women, Charles," he said, "is that they're free to despise us. It's a risk I find unacceptable."

Charles glared at him, pale with fury. William sighed. Since their most recent break, their friendship stood on shakier ground than before. William used to know precisely what would anger Charles and how far he could push or tease him. But Frankenstein's emotions burned on a shorter fuse since he brought Eva into his house. William supposed that soon Charles would take his protégée to wife. After that, inevitably, his life as a family man would diverge from Clerval's as a sworn bachelor, and their friendship would finally slip away.

On the other hand, a great tension existed between Eva and Charles. Perhaps he would send her back to wherever she came from. Perhaps she would leave him. Nothing Eva did would surprise Clerval.

Eva marched into the library, stopped in front of Charles, and flung a book at his feet. As she turned to go she fixed her angry gaze on Clerval, as if daring him, no, *willing* him, to take Charles's part in the argument. Her eyes flashed violet, lit by an inner power that chilled Clerval and shattered his deliberate nonchalance. Eva stormed from the library again, slamming the door behind her. Both men stared after her.

Clerval picked up the book. He looked at its spine.

"*Prometheus,* by Shelley," he said. "Who *is* she, Charles? Who *is* she?"

Charles shook himself forcibly from his shock. "What on earth do you mean?" he said sharply.

"Sometimes, Charles . . . she hasn't a woman's eyes." He stroked his finger along the gold lettering of the book. "Sometimes . . . she hasn't human eyes."

Charles said nothing for some moments. William had the sense of a great weight of words building up within his friend, words that needed to be spoken to lance the pressure of an invisible guilt. But the words never came. Instead, Charles rose, took the book very gently from William's hands, read the spine for himself, and smiled.

"Let *me* ask *you* a question, William," he said. He riffled the pages casually. Then he snapped it shut and tossed it carelessly into the fireplace.

It fell with a hollow thump, a soft cloud of ashes, and then the heat curled its edges and it burst into a flame that Clerval thought must be as brilliant as the light of man's original Promethean fire.

"Whose *Prometheus* is it now?" Charles asked. He paused, but his friend had no reply. "Whose name is written on those ashes?"

William Clerval prided himself on his imperturbability.

He shivered.

Nightmares continued to trouble Eva's sleep. She woke that night, thinking she heard the sound of thunder. But the sky was clear. A light crust of snow reflected the brilliance of stars and the full moon. Eva huddled beneath the feather bed, but the chill penetrated to her bones. Finally she flung away the covers, dressed herself, and stole from the castle.

A few minutes later her gray mare galloped from the courtyard, carrying her toward the dawn.

She reached Brucor at midday. On the single street of the small and isolated village, the children ran after her. They tried to keep pace but quickly fell behind. They stared after her, wide-eyed at the sight of a lady on an Arabian horse, a lady all alone.

She reached her destination, dismounted, and knocked at a small cottage. After a time, the door opened. A stooped, wizened man in spectacles peered at her shortsightedly.

"Are you the doctor in this village?" Eva asked.

"Yes, I am," he said. He regarded her with curiosity and calculation. "And what can I do for *you?*"

"I want to ask you about the girl that was brought to you, the one found in the forest."

"Girl?" the doctor said, completely baffled.

"Yes. The one who lost her memory."

"No one's brought such a girl to me," he said. "I've been here forty years, and no one's brought me such a girl."

"Is there another doctor in Brucor?"

"Oh, no. Not another for miles."

"Do you recognize me?"

"No," the doctor said.

"Thank you, then," Eva said, restraining disappointment and anger so she would not unleash them upon this innocent old man.

"I also pull teeth," the doctor said hopefully.

Without replying, Eva mounted her horse and rode away.

Chapter 11

Viktor trudged along the cold, dusty road, retracing his and Rinaldo's route to Budapest. He had been walking for—he could not quite recall how long. He stopped only when exhaustion prevented his taking another step. Crawling among tree roots or beneath bushes to sleep had made a wreck of his clothes, but he could hardly bring himself to care. His appearance had made no difference to anyone in the world but Rinaldo, and Rinaldo was gone.

He reached into his pocket and closed his fingers around the necklace Rinaldo had given him, his only token of his only friend, the only remnant of Rinaldo's dream.

Rinaldo's assurances kept returning to him. Follow your heart, Rinaldo had said. Trust your dream. Approach her slowly, softly. You frightened her before: take more care this time.

A brightly-painted Gypsy cart stood by the side of the road ahead. Its unharnessed horses cropped the sparse grass, and its driver sat dozing in the wan winter sun. Viktor touched Rinaldo's token as if it were a good-luck charm, and, like a charm, it gave him courage.

He stopped beside the peddler and prodded him gently. The man woke, muttering and mumbling.

"Needles, pins, fine thread, hard candy. Feathers and decorations—Aieeeee!" He screamed when he saw Viktor and tried to run away.

"No!" Viktor said urgently. His voice was even more

cracked and hoarse than before. His cries to Rinaldo, in the ring, had damaged it permanently. But since that night, though it made uglier sounds, it gave him less pain. "No! Buy. Buy!"

Instead of fleeing, the peddler regained his composure.

"Buy, eh? Why didn't you say so?" He hurried to the back of his wagon and opened the doors, revealing bolts of ribbon, skeins of lace. "What exactly did you have in mind?" the peddler asked.

"For ladies," Viktor said.

"Something for the ladies. My friend, you're in luck today. I have in this van the largest selection of baubles and sanitary sundries known on the continent of Europe. What will it be? Silks, accessories, ornaments?"

"Sparkles," Viktor said.

"Jewels! And don't I have them!" The peddler reached into the van and pulled out a handful of necklaces and bracelets. They glittered as if they reflected a bright summer sun.

Viktor smiled. They reflected the beauty of the woman he cherished.

"Just like diamonds and rubies, eh?" the peddler said. "I won't say they *are* diamonds and rubies—I won't even say they're anything but cut glass. But don't they sparkle, sir? Don't they shine?"

"How much?" Viktor asked, entranced.

"How much," the peddler said cautiously, "have you got?"

Viktor pulled out the pouch of gold coins. Rinaldo had said it would be enough to take them to their dreams. He opened it and poured the coins into his hand.

"Oh . . . I imagine it would take most of that," the peddler said.

Viktor offered him the gold. The peddler took the coins,

leaving one in Viktor's hand. Viktor thought him kind to leave it, though he did not know what he would do with it. He did not need to exchange gold for the acorns he ate or for the hollow trees in which he slept.

The peddler glanced at Viktor, sidelong, fearful. Viktor felt sad to have frightened him. He wondered what he had done. Perhaps the peddler was too afraid to take a fair price for his wares. Viktor hopefully offered him the last gold coin.

The peddler took it, then poured all the other gold coins back into Viktor's hand.

"One will do," he said, and when Viktor looked at the mound of gold in confusion, the peddler gestured for him to keep it.

"Thank you," Viktor said.

The peddler handed him the bracelet and the necklace.

"I hope she likes them," he said.

Viktor touched the diamond-clear glass of the bracelet, the ruby-red and emerald-green glass of the necklace.

"Thank you," he said again.

He left the peddler and continued along the road, a new spring to his step, new hope in his heart. Every few yards he touched the jewels in his pocket; every few miles he took them out to look at them again. And so the hours and the distance passed more quickly than before.

Eva fidgeted in the carriage, wishing she were riding her gray mare. In the same time it took the carriage to convey her to town and bring her home, she could have visited the seamstress and spent the afternoon riding in the mountains. She would still have had ample time to bathe and dress and make final preparations for the masquerade ball. But Frankenstein claimed it was not proper for her to ride into town on horseback; if she were to go at all she must take the carriage. She complied with his wishes in order to avoid a painful argument.

Eva looked forward to the evening. The party was her idea; Charles had only agreed to it because Clerval teased him for his rudeness in accepting other invitations while offering none of his own. Charles had never seemed terribly pleased about being a host; and as the date neared he had become more and more nervous and edgy, more and more difficult.

Ever since the argument over Shelley's *Prometheus,* he seemed angry all the time. His wishes had become almost impossible to comprehend. Once, trying to joke, Eva told him that she found considerable irony in being reprimanded for improper behavior by someone who had been dismissed from university for the same offense. Infuriated, he flung a crystal wineglass across the library. The red wine stained a row of books and a fine Chinese carpet.

Only when Hannah complimented her on her ability to divine his wishes and get what she wanted anyway, did Eva realize how much she had circumscribed her own behavior. The more she tried to please him, the more demanding he became, the more mercurial his moods. When she could not discover what he wanted, he would never tell her; he seemed to prefer to shout abuse. And on those occasions when she went her own way—which had become rarer and rarer without her noticing it—he retaliated by locking himself into the library for hours or days at a time, refusing food, and finally emerging pale and shaky and reeking of the pungent smoky odor that so often filled the castle.

Eva did not know what to do. She admired him, she respected him, she believed she loved him. She wanted to help him, but the harder she tried, the further he withdrew.

Viktor stopped. A hay wagon lay sideways across the road before him. The farmer pushed and grunted and tried to right it. On the other side of the wagon, a coachman shouted for the farmer to get out of the way and let him pass.

Viktor grabbed the wagon's side and heaved it upright.

The farmer leaped aboard, chirruped to his horses, and drove out of the way. The coachman cracked his whip. As the carriage rumbled past, Viktor glanced curiously through the window.

He stared after the carriage, unable to move till it had vanished. The woman within—it was *she!* She who had been made to be his friend, she whom he had terrified with his clumsy abruptness.

She was so different! For the first instant he had not recognized her. Her hair was different, and her clothing. But he entertained no uncertainty whatsoever about her identity.

After the carriage had passed, the farmer pulled his wagon to a halt and glanced back at Viktor.

"Thanks, stranger," he said. "You saved me from a horse-whipping, it may be. Are you going my direction?"

Viktor shook his head.

"Then, good-bye, and good luck to you." The farmer tsked to his horses, and the wagon rumbled down the rutted road.

Viktor set off across the field again, taking the shortest way through the forest to Castle Frankenstein.

He reached his destination when the shadows of late afternoon stretched long across the earth. He spied on the castle until he saw movement in a window several stories above the ground. He crept forward silently. Ivy grew thickly over the castle wall, its vines nearly the thickness of Viktor's wrists. He tested them gingerly, and found they would bear his weight.

He climbed.

Once the mortar crumbled as he grasped the tendril burrowing into it. A great swath of ivy tore away. He snatched at a stronger vine and saved himself a fall. Finally his fingers curled around the windowsill. He levered himself up and cautiously peered within.

She sat in a tub with her back to him, stretching luxuriously like a cat. A second young woman bathed her with a large sea sponge. The soapsuds slid down her silken skin. Then she stood, and the serving woman poured a bucket of steaming clean water over her to rinse the soapsuds away. The maid took a large towel from a rack before the fire and wrapped her in it.

Viktor watched with wonder. He wished he could simply look at her forever. The ivy sagged beneath his weight, ripping gradually from the wall. He grabbed the vines on the other side of the window and continued watching.

She was magnificent. She glowed as brightly as her eyes. The maid covered her luminous skin, dressing her in lacy white clothing more complicated than any costume he had ever seen, more complicated even than Rinaldo's harness. Maid and mistress chattered and laughed together. The ancient glass was too thick for Viktor to hear anything of what they said. The women moved from the bathing chamber through a doorway and out of his sight.

The vines finally gave way.

Viktor clutched at the wall and caught himself. He moved awkwardly sideways. His fingers ached, but he no more could have climbed down now than he could fly. He reached the next window and looked inside.

The woman stepped into a blue satin dress almost worthy of her. The serving woman fastened it, then combed out her long lustrous hair and pinned it into complicated curls.

Viktor thought of the jewels in his pocket. He wished he

could give them to her now! The blue glass in the necklace would certainly—almost surely—nearly—match the color of her dress.

The woman opened an ornate box on the table before her and drew out a ruby necklace.

Viktor gasped.

The rubies glowed against her throat, pulsing as if her life's blood gave them animation. But she shook her head and laid them aside and then drew out a string of sapphires, the blue of mountain skies. She held them to her throat. Yet again she shook her head, laid the jewels aside, and reached into her magical box.

The diamonds possessed no color of their own. Their crystal clarity captured the firelight. They spun it into rainbows, into the wings of butterflies and hummingbirds.

The woman fastened the diamond necklace around her throat, a bracelet on her wrist, long sparkling earrings on her ears.

Viktor nearly lost his hold on the ivy. HIs heavy boots scraped along the stones, tearing the vines away. He tumbled to the ground. He froze, afraid he had made so much noise that he must be discovered. He pressed himself against the wall, trying to conceal himself among the inadequate shadows. But if anyone heard him, they did not sound an alarm.

Affected for the first time by his exhaustion, disgusted with himself, with his own stupidity, Viktor tramped across the castle grounds and into the forest.

He walked until he reached a small, deep mountain lake. He sat down and stared into the water. After a long while, he reached into his pocket and drew out the glass jewels.

The ornaments that had so affected him with their color now appeared dull and ugly. He had carried them in his pocket for many miles, and some of the fittings were bent and broken. His pocket was full of sharp glass shards. One pricked his finger, drawing blood. He barely noticed.

Viktor smiled sadly and shook his head at his own stupidity, his naivete. Even Rinaldo's wisdom had failed him. His eyes full of tears, Viktor cried out in grief and flung the beads into the lake. They sank, leaving nothing but ripples behind.

As the last few minutes before the masquerade slipped away, Charles Frankenstein prowled his castle like a nervous cat. Even opium failed to calm him. He had planned the decorations carefully; the castle resembled Venice during carnival. At the same time, his home had been transformed from a dark and comfortable sanctuary to a bright, gaudy, alien place.

Eva swept down the stairs in a magnificent new dress of blue satin. She wore his diamonds. Her eyes were more brilliant. She paused a few steps above him. He had an instant's impulse to reach out to her and take her away where they could be alone. But the wretched masquerade—no doubt Eva would say they must welcome their guests.

When Charles did not speak to her, Eva smiled enigmatically and raised her domino to cover her eyes.

Carriage wheels rattled on the cobblestones outside. Eva hurried past him to greet the first arrivals.

Eva felt as if she embraced the whole universe, as if she held its beauty and power in her hands. The castle lay transformed around her, changed from a quiet, gloomy, outdated old house to a magic crystal palace. The orchestra, all in white, tuned their instruments. Notes in curious harmony fluttered through the hall. The gathering guests left bare the center of the gleaming parquet floor and waited for the dancing to begin.

Eva glanced at Charles. He saw her, but pretended not to. Her happiness diminished. She had hoped—in vain—that he might enjoy the masquerade once it began.

He leaned languidly against the mantel, chatting desultorily with a man disguised as a satyr. Eva recognized William Clerval by the line of his jaw, the slightly sardonic curve of his lips. And the nature of the mask hinted at his identity, with its devilish ears, high arched brows, its rams-horns, and its curiously evil yellow eyes with their horizontal pupils.

Charles wore a simpler mask, one made of a long white strip of satin tied at the back of his head. The white silk seemed hardly less pale than his complexion. Though he toyed idly with the stem of a full goblet, he never put his lips to the red wine.

Eva moved to his side and brushed her fingers across the back of his hand. Its icy coldness intensified her concern for him. He glanced at her sharply, and she caught her breath. His eyes seemed more eerie than the goat eyes of Clerval's mask. Only the faintest rim of crystalline blue outlined his pupils. He was so beautiful and vulnerable that for an instant Eva nearly threw herself at his feet; she nearly cried, Tell me your pain, so I may take it from you; tell me what I must do to make you love me as I love you!

But she did and said nothing of the sort, knowing it would embarrass him, knowing it would drive him at best to silence, at worst to shutting himself away in the library again.

Instead, she grasped his cold hand, pretending nothing at all was wrong.

"Come, Charles," she said. "The orchestra is ready, and we must begin the dancing."

He twisted his hand from hers.

"You know I do not dance," he said.

"We need not do a difficult step—"

"I do not dance!"

"But no one will begin before we do. It isn't proper."

He scowled at what she meant as gentle teasing.

"You wished to have this ball, my dear. My responsibility ended with paying for it. It is now your responsibility."

The orchestra struck up a few notes of the first dance, but when no one moved onto the floor, the conductor stopped the music. Clerval turned his masked face away, but Eva knew he, and anyone else nearby, could not help but listen.

Eva recalled how she had seen other women persuade men to do their bidding. She had decided it must be a small social game to be played at salons and parties. But she had never played it herself, for as far as she could recall, this was the first time anyone at any gathering had ever refused her smallest whim.

Perhaps Charles wanted her to play the small social games with him.

She looked him in the eyes and slowly batted her eyelashes at him. She leaned toward him, kissed her fingertip, and brushed the kiss against his cheek.

"But, Charles—"

To her dismay and confusion, he drew back from her touch.

The orchestra began again; it stopped again.

"At least try to comport yourself like a lady!" he snarled, his teeth clenched.

"My dear Charles!" William said, shocked.

Eva felt the blood rush from her cheeks. She bit her lip to still its trembling: she *would not* show how much his rejection hurt her.

Can I do nothing to win back your approval? she thought. What did I do to lose it?

"You wanted to have this ball," Charles said with a nasty

hint of satisfaction, as if he had been saving his speech for a long time. "You knew someone must begin the dancing; you know I do not dance. I never agreed to make a fool of myself out there for your amusement. Unlike you, my dear, *I* do not promise things that are beyond my ability to give."

He turned back to Clerval.

For a third time, the orchestra began playing, with an urgent, ragged intensity.

Eva felt suddenly as if she were engulfed in a bolt of angry light. She grabbed Clerval's hand and drew him toward the center of the ballroom floor.

"If I am not to be chosen, I must choose. William, will you condescend to take your best friend's place?"

"Gladly," the satyr said in a stunned voice. Clerval gathered her into his arms and swept her into the steps. The music strengthened, steadied, and soared.

"Thank you," Eva said, when they had spun once around the hall, when other couples had joined them. "I apologize—"

William laughed shakily. "No need," he said. "I've known him far longer than you, remember. I'm used to his moods, I recognize them." He chuckled again, ruefully this time. "I recognize this one. I'll have to be double my usual charming and witty self to return to his good graces."

"I did not mean to apologize for him," Eva said, "but for me. For my . . . improper behavior."

"You behaved in no way improperly," William said.

"But Charles—"

"Charles, for all his brilliance, is a prig and a fool about certain subjects," William said. He paused, then thought better of whatever he was about to tell her. "I say, Eva, how did you know it was me? I thought this was a damned fine mask."

"Mask?" Eva said innocently. "Why, Monsieur Clerval—are you wearing a mask?"

Laughing, she threw herself into the dance.

William Clerval could still feel Eva's strength and excitement, tingling through his hands. She had spun across the floor and he had been lost in the dazzle of her diamonds and the depths of her incredible eyes. When the music stopped, she was still fresh, he short of breath. Half jealous, half grateful, he let her go to a new partner.

Clerval loved masquerades. Talking Charles into holding one had been much easier than he expected, though he did feel a trifle guilty that Eva was reaping the blame for it.

Now she stood on the other side of the candlelit room, looking like the queen of Faerie. She was a mythic power, a power the elements of the universe came to serve. Earth and air, water and fire, she commanded them all. When she had glared at Charles, candlelight sparkled from the diamonds on her mask. For an instant she looked like a goddess with lightning in her eyes.

As the orchestra struck up a lively tune, Josef Schildman, uniformed and masked, made his way to Eva's side and whispered something in her ear. She laughed—not a simpering, flattering giggle, but a real laugh—put her hand to his cheek, and danced away with him.

Josef had been paying his attentions to her since the first time he saw her, at the countess's; William had watched his progress with endless fascination. Josef, while a pleasant enough young man, and certainly well set up, had hardly a brain in his head. He was known to be fickle. William wondered if Eva knew what she wanted in those matters as well as she did in more intellectual pursuits. Once William asked Charles some roundabout question concerning Eva and Josef, and Charles pretended not to know what he was talking about. Worse than that, he pretended to believe Eva could have no interest in the subject unless he presented it to her. For all his cant about freedom and independence, he had yet to realize how free and independent Eva was. The fact that Charles continued to neglect various facets of her education did not necessarily mean Eva had not set her own lesson plan.

For his own part, William felt relieved that Eva kept a distance between them. She frightened him, though he could not have said why. Worse, she would not react to contempt with self-effacement, or to condescension with a further effort to please, as other women did. She kept him off balance, and this he disliked intensely. One dance with her—however intoxicating it had been—was quite as close as he cared to come.

Josef Schildman swept her past. Clerval suddenly realized that her mask bore no diamonds. . . .

Enough about the mysterious Miss Eva! he thought. I intend to have some fun tonight!

Wearing his excellent mask, he capered across the ballroom and between the dancers, pausing now and again to cock his head at a lady and let his painted satyr's face leer and tease.

Eva put Josef Schildman's name on her dance card when he threatened to beg on his knees for a dance, but the truth was that he did not have to beg at all. She liked him; he made no pretense of great intellect and therefore did not keep watch continually for challenges to his perceived superiority. Eva did not have to prove herself worthy to speak each time they met, as she did with most of Charles's acquaintances. And she found him attractive. He roused her curiosity.

She danced with him, enjoying the sensation of their bodies moving together, touching now and again. She looked into his eyes, which were blue and clear. He met her gaze— he always seemed a little shocked that she would look him straight in the eye. At first her directness had made him nervous, but as he grew more accustomed to it, it began to have a different effect. Now he found it entrancing, challenging, provoking. They smiled at each other, held each other closer, and whirled across the floor.

William, bored for the moment with leering and teasing, paused among other onlookers. Beside him stood a gentleman in an eagle's head mask that completely concealed his identity.

"My word, what a magnificent mask," William said. "Who is beneath it?"

"That would be telling," the eagle said.

"Why, Leo," William said, recognizing the voice, "not dancing?"

"You might at least pretend to be fooled by my disguise," Leo said. He shrugged with exaggerated self-pity. "Grete refused to give me every dance, and I don't care to dance with any other."

"Ah, I see," William said, nodding. "Unrequited love. You need something to distract you. I say, Leo, wouldn't it be fun to trade masks for an hour? Come on, damned good fun."

Leo allowed himself to be persuaded, and so the satyr took on the disguise of an eagle.

Charles Frankenstein had always concerned himself with much more important matters than learning to dance. He felt he had been right to rebuke Eva. But since she danced away with William Clerval, she had barely paused to nod to Charles. He felt lonely and a little put out. He rather wished he had taken up her challenge, or at least turned it down more gracefully.

Now he could not find her at all; one moment she had been in the midst of the revelers, the next she was gone. He wandered along the edges of the party, barely acknowledging the compliments of his guests. His loneliness pained him. If Eva did not want to dance anymore, she should have come to keep him company, to talk to him.

He wandered through the castle, ignoring the couples who stood half concealed in shadows and masks, who moved in ways better kept private.

The door to the library, which he himself had closed, stood ajar. He had opened nearly the whole of his house to his guests, yet they must take more. Mere acquaintances had invaded his library, where he kept certain books of which the authorities disapproved.

He entered the library, to make some excuse and ask the intruders to leave.

The heavy drapes opened wide to let in moonlight that illuminated the room, glowing against leather bindings and gold lettering, sliding like the sea across the oak table. Charles seldom opened the drapes in the library. But as he stepped forward to close them, he saw Eva.

She had not yet noticed him, for she sat in a bright pool of moonlight and he remained in the shadows by the door. Perched next to her on the edge of the sofa, Josef Schildman leaned toward her intently. They spoke in low tones. Charles could not discern the topic of their conversation. But there was no impropriety whatever in their position or their actions, nothing but innocence in Eva's smile or in her laugh, even in her quick touch to Josef's hand.

They had put aside their disguises. On the floor by their feet, their shadow-eyed masks lay one atop the other.

His heart pounding, Charles moved behind the door and

out of their sight. Near fainting, he leaned against the wall.
His nails scraped against the cool stone, grasping at its
strength and solidity. But within himself he felt only heat,
confusion, and unreasoning jealousy. Eva's flirtatiousness
was purely innocent, the game of a little girl copying her coy
older sisters. He knew that. His reaction was absurd.

And yet his jealousy intensified.

The beak of Leo's eagle mask pressed against Grete's
throat. William Clerval folded his arms around her from
behind, nuzzled the curve of her neck and shoulder, and
nibbled her earlobe.

"Oh, Leo," she whispered.

Beneath Leo's mask, Clerval tried not to laugh and give
his game away.

Laughing and flushed as the lively dance ended, Eva applauded the orchestra. Josef Schildman appeared at her elbow.

"My dance, I believe," he said to Count Malvas, who
despite his age and infirmities had insisted on partnering
Eva for this dance. He looked all the better for it.

"Were I truly as young as you have made me feel, my
dear," the count said to Eva, "I might wrestle this pup for
the pleasure of your company. But I am not, so my only
choice is to retire gracefully from the lists." He bowed over
Eva's hand.

Josef enfolded Eva and danced her away. He guided her
toward the entranceway of the great hall.

"Spiriting her off again, eh, Schildman?" said another
young officer from Josef's brigade.

"Envy does not become you, Oskar," Josef said pleasantly. He led Eva from the great hall.

"Where are you going?" she asked.

"Why—back to the library."

One of the footmen came by with a tray; Josef took two glasses of champagne and handed one to Eva.

"And," he said, "I thought you might be thirsty."

Eva sipped the champagne. She liked the way the bubbles prickled against her tongue; she liked the light-headed feeling it brought her.

"Josef," she said, "I don't understand why you beg me to dance, then insist on sitting in the library while the dance is going on."

"It wasn't the dance I wanted, so much as to be with you," Josef said. "That's what balls are for, after all—excuses to spend time with those for whom one has . . ." He hesitated. ". . . deeper feelings."

"Do we need excuses?"

He did not answer for a moment. Eva had the impression that he had been hoping she would say something different, but that he was not entirely disappointed by what she did say.

"Of course we do," he said. "Otherwise, people would talk. People might . . . object."

"What would they talk about? To what would they object? Who are these 'people'?" she asked, baffled.

"They would think we were behaving with impropriety."

"But surely we are not responsible for what people think?"

He met her direct gaze. "For all his advanced ideas, your guardian might not like us to be alone together."

Eva frowned curiously. "What does Frankenstein have to do with you and me?"

"He is responsible for you—"

Her temper flared. "*I* am responsible for myself!" Angrily she strode into the sitting room and stared into the fire, sipping her champagne and trying to make sense of what Josef had said.

She felt him, the warmth and presence of him, at her elbow. She did not turn. He took her empty glass, put it on the mantelpiece, and handed her a full goblet.

"I have so much to learn!" she said. "I know so little of life—"

"The Baron is a scholar," Josef said. "He knows everything about natural philosophy. But scholars live secluded from the world, so he knows only a little of life. Nevertheless, I think he would dislike your taking any other teacher."

"I will choose my own teachers, if I please!"

"Would you," he said softly, his voice much changed, "choose me?"

She leaned over and kissed him quickly, lightly, on the cheek.

Suddenly Charles was at her side. His fingers clamped around her elbow and he pulled her around, so quickly she was too surprised to resist.

"You've had quite enough to drink this evening," he said. His voice was cold, his pupils dilated so wide that his eyes looked black. "I think it's time you retired."

Defiant, Eva met his angry gaze. "Very well," she said. She turned to their guests, freeing her arm from his grip. "My friends," she said, not loudly, but in a voice that stilled the laughs and chatter. "My guardian says it is time for me to retire, so I must bid you all good night."

Of the guests, only Josef remained silent. He looked too angry to speak. The others protested Eva's departure.

"Charles," said a gargoyle mask with the voice of William Clerval, "don't be a beast." He pushed the mask to the top of his head so Charles could see his face, and his smile. "After all, we came to see her—not you."

Everyone laughed, except Charles. He paled suddenly. Though she still felt angry at him, Eva took a step toward him, afraid he would faint. But he withdrew; he glared at her, at Josef, at William.

"Very well," he said, his voice tight. "Suit yourselves."

He turned abruptly and strode from the room.

Eva felt both sorry for angering him, and triumphant. The two opposing emotions confused her.

Josef touched her arm. It was a much gentler touch than Charles's, and, right now, much more welcome.

"What a damnable bore!" Josef said so only Eva could hear.

Indeed, Charles sometimes *was* a bore. He grew angry at a joke from his oldest friend, a joke easily deflected with a laugh. He had looked so funny, glaring at Clerval as if the mild jibe were mortal insult. Eva could not help it: she giggled.

William rather wished that he had not made the jest at Charles's expense, but Charles should know by now that he could never let pass any opportunity for a joke. Besides, the hour was late and Clerval, like everyone else, was a little drunk. As for Charles—Charles had barely taken a drop of wine all evening. He seemed to be using something stronger these days, despite his disapproval of "Oriental morals." William guessed that he had taken to opium.

On the other side of the room, a lady with whom William had been trying to further his acquaintance—rather successfully, in fact—suddenly ripped Clerval's satyr's mask from Leo's head and slapped Leo soundly across the face.

"You deceitful wretch!" she exclaimed. Her cheeks flushed scarlet. Clerval had the distinct impression that her exclamation was directed at someone other than Leo.

There's a joke on me, Clerval thought, and could not help

but smile. But it would be a joke no longer if the lady in question found him while she was in her present state of outrage. He turned his back quickly and sidled up beside Josef, who watched bereft as the gentleman to whom Eva had promised the next dance took her away on his arm.

"I say, Josef, wouldn't it be amusing to switch masks for an hour or so? Come on, damned good fun."

Josef shrugged and switched masks. Smiling within the safety of his new disguise, Clerval sauntered off toward the dancers, leaving Josef to take the brunt of Clerval's lady's annoyance.

Chapter 12

By dawn, the last guests had departed. Eva's mask, on her dressing table, seemed to wink at her. She did not feel tired, but she felt sad.

The castle lay silent around her. She had bid farewell to the guests all alone. She had not seen Charles since their disagreement, and when she tried the library door, it was locked.

Perhaps if she left him alone, his moodiness would pass. She dressed, went to the stable, saddled her mare, and rode out into the frosty morning.

She rode all the way to the abbey. She always felt comfortable and happy there, despite its isolation. She was glad everyone in the valley believed the road dangerous. When she needed solitude, she found it here. The rectory lay against the mountainside like a dragon asleep since antediluvian times, and the wind sang in the stones. She liked to wander through the cemetery, wondering about her ancestry with a pleasurable sadness.

But today a thin curl of smoke rose from the lantern above the crypt.

She dismounted and approached its entrance. At the bottom of the stairs, a man sat in silhouette against the dim light of a tiny fire. On the ground before him, a still pool of water reflected his face.

He turned, startled. His clothes were ragged, his face haggard and sad.

"What are you doing here?" she asked.

"Going now," he said. He would have bolted up the stairs, but Eva was standing in his path.

"Have you no other place to sleep?" She had not intended to frighten him or drive him away. The sadness in his eyes touched her heart.

"Going . . . on the road." Though his voice was harsh and low, it was not unpleasant, perhaps because he so clearly must put great effort into his speech.

"I didn't mean to startle you," she said. "Where are you going?"

"Far," he said. "Far away . . . from men."

"Someplace unknown?" A moment ago she had pitied him; now she almost envied him. To be free to go anywhere—

"Where men don't go."

"Like the Congo," she said, imagining. "Or South America . . ."

He shook his head, unable to explain. "Yes," he said.

"You have quite a long journey ahead of you, then," Eva said. "You might need this." She reached into her cloak and drew out a coin, which she offered to him.

He looked at it and shook his head.

"Go on," Eva said. "Take it—for luck."

She pressed it into his hand. He raised his head and looked directly into her eyes.

Eva pulled back, startled by the clarity of his gaze. No one had ever met her eyes so directly.

"Godspeed to you, sir," she said. She turned and hurried from the crypt, confused by her own emotions, feeling foolish to be frightened for no reason.

"Wait."

The harsh voice stopped her. She spun around. The man loomed over her. Standing above him on the stairs, she had not realized how tall he was. She looked up at him, pierced by his stare.

He reached up. He opened his frayed collar, drew a gold chain over his head, and handed it to her. Her fingers clenched around it. She felt the cool links of the chain, the round smoothness of a charm, but she could not look away from his eyes. He never took his gaze from her face.

"Why are you looking at me that way?" A faint memory tugged at her, but she could not catch it, she could not identify it. "Have I seen you before?" she asked.

Then, finally, he broke the connection between them. He lowered his head and looked at the frozen ground.

"No," he said softly.

And Eva knew he lied. She *knew* he lied; she knew he had known her from the time she could not remember, and his recollection was so horrible that he could not speak it. She fled from him, she fled from the time before.

She ran to her horse and snatched up the reins. But her agitation frightened the gray mare, who snorted and shied. The mare tugged at the reins, watching her sidelong, ready to rear and kick.

Eva, trembling, stood very still. She held the mare's soft muzzle and breathed gently into her nostrils. The horse calmed just long enough to let her mount, then bolted down the trail.

Eva still felt displaced and unsettled when she returned to Castle Frankenstein. She wanted to go to her room and rest and think.

She opened the door and entered.

"Where have you been all day?"

Halfway down the staircase, Charles paused. At midafternoon he was still in his dressing-gown. His hair was uncombed, his face pale, his eyes black.

"Riding," she said shortly.

She still held clenched in her hand the gold chain, which she had nearly forgotten. Without thinking, she hid it behind her. Scowling, Charles descended the stairs two at a time.

"What have you got there?"

She had no reason to hide it. She brought her hand from behind her back and opened her clenched fingers.

"I saw a strange man at the monastery, a poor wretch who was passing along the road."

Charles sneered. "Are you sure it wasn't your cavalry officer—'lost' again?"

"What are you talking about?"

"A little token, from one of your many admirers."

He grabbed the chain and held it up. It was brass and pot-metal. A crude gondola sailed across the circular charm. "He certainly has poor taste—whoever he is." Frankenstein shook the chain scornfully.

Eva snatched it back, infuriated by his contempt.

"Don't speak to me that way! How dare you!"

"How dare *I?*"

Eva burst into furious tears, pushed past him, and fled up the stairs. She ran into her room and flung herself onto her bed.

"Miss Eva! What's wrong?" Hannah hurried from the dressing room.

Eva sat up, dashing the tears angrily from her cheeks, embarrassed to be seen crying.

"I—I thought you had already gone. To your mother's."

"Miss Eva, did he hurt you? What happened?" Hannah took her hands to comfort her. The tarnished chain clinked. Eva put the necklace into her pocket.

"I cannot stay here," she said.

"But, Miss—where would you go?"

"You must take a note to town for me before you stop at your mother's."

"I won't leave you, all upset like this!"

"You must, Hannah. Please."

"Don't make me. Let me go with you."

"I cannot. I have no money, I don't know what will happen."

"If you leave this place, I won't stay, either."

"But—"

"I won't!" Hannah cried in distress. She jumped to her feet. "I'll never go back to being a scullery maid!"

Eva wiped her face on her sleeve and regained some of her composure.

"You needn't, Hannah—of course you needn't! Why, half the ladies in town—ladies far more fashionable than I— have hinted they'd steal you away in an instant. I've told you that."

"I don't want to work for them. I want to work for you."

"But you do not work for me, dear Hannah. You work for the Baron. And I cannot stay in his house any longer."

Tears ran down Hannah's cheeks.

"What will you do? What will I do?"

"You will deliver my note for me, then visit your mother as you always do. But tomorrow, instead of coming back here, you will take the letter I write for you and apply for a position anywhere you like."

Her fair complexion reddened by weeping, Hannah sniffled and stared at the floor.

"Hannah," Eva said. "You must."

"I know, Miss," she whispered.

At nightfall, Viktor trudged into a town. He ignored the stares and whispers of the citizens, for he was used to all that by now. He thought about what had happened back at the monastery, about what *she* had said. The Congo? South America? The exotic words brought visions of places where he might escape and be alone and at peace. One could reach them by ship; he wondered if his gold coins would be enough to pay for his passage.

Near a fountain on the commons, a familiar poster brought him up short: Magar's Traveling Carnival. Wild animals and clowns, hilarity and danger.

Viktor looked around in terror. He had not expected to cross paths with the carnival; he had not thought to hide. Many people had seen him as he wandered through their town. Magar might have described him and warned everyone that he was dangerous; he might have told them that Viktor should be captured and killed. He must flee into the wilderness—

"There he is!"

A pack of villagers, carrying lanterns and torches, clubs and staves, pounded toward him across the green.

Viktor fled. Another hunting party rounded a corner and spied him. They threatened him with clubs and torches.

Viktor's power gave him no advantage in a chase where he needed speed. He cut across the commons and lumbered into an alley between dark high stone walls. His feet crunched on the half-frozen surface of the open drain.

Panting, searching desperately for a place of concealment, Viktor stumbled farther and farther into the black warrens of the town. The shouts and cries of the hunting party receded. He huddled in a deeply recessed doorway.

From the end of the alley came a soft, hesitant tapping. Viktor held his breath and made himself stay very still.

An elderly man, feeling his way with a cane, walked toward him.

Rinaldo was right, Viktor thought. I do have a heart. It is beating so hard that it will betray me.

The elderly blind man passed him, his feet scuffing on the cobblestones. Viktor dared to hope he would escape.

The old man stopped. Viktor pressed himself against the rough planks of the door. The old man turned toward him, his head cocked to one side. He reached out and touched Viktor's shoulder, slid his hand to Viktor's face, and read his features with his hand. He smiled. Viktor let his breath out in a sigh of relief. So not all men feared and hated him—

"Help! Here he is! Here he is! I've found him!" the blind man cried, his voice high and loud and shocking.

Viktor fled again, but the villagers came at him from both ends of the alley. They thrust torches into his face. He ran a few steps this way, a few steps that. Flames stopped him. He made a low, frightened sound. The townspeople pressed him into a corner with their torches. He cringed from their fire, and the exulting people surrounded him with ropes and nets. They tied him, prodded him to see him flinch from the heat, and led him away.

Charles stared into the flames of the candles that lit the dining room. He had not seen Eva since this afternoon, since their argument. He expected her to have returned, by now, to her usual good humor.

Hearing footsteps, he glanced up. Mrs. Baumann put a plate of soup before him.

"She isn't coming down?"

"No, sir," Mrs. Baumann said.

"Go and fetch her!"

"Sir, I—"

"Go and fetch her, I say!"

"I can't, sir, she's—"

"What in blazes!"

"She isn't here, milord."

Charles leaped to his feet. His heavy chair scraped backward across the floor.

"Where is she?"

"Sir, I don't know, oh, sir, she—"

In a fury, Charles grabbed Mrs. Baumann by the wrist.

"Tell me where she is, by God, or I'll break your arm!"

Mrs. Baumann struggled and burst into tears. He tightened his grip and shook her.

"She left in a carriage, sir. She—"

"Whose carriage?"

She sobbed so violently that she could not speak. Charles shook her to silence.

"*Whose?*"

"Colonel Schildman's, milord. She made me swear—"

Charles shoved her away from him.

"You will leave this house immediately, Mrs. Baumann. Your employment here is ended."

He stormed from the room.

Viktor let the villagers drag him into the dungeon and chain him to the wall. He could have resisted; he supposed he could have killed several of them. But he saw no reason to fight. *She* was forever beyond his reach, and Rinaldo was dead. He was too tired for more struggle. Shackles clamped him against the weeping stone; and Viktor wept, too.

Magar strode into the dungeon and looked him up and down. Suddenly he slapped Viktor across the face. Viktor gasped and jerked away in surprise.

"That's for Bela," Magar said. His lips twisted in a snarl. He slapped Viktor even harder. "And that's for me."

Viktor tasted warm salty blood from his split lip. He had nothing to say. His tortured words had done him no good in the past. He only wished that whatever the men planned, they would carry it out and be done with it, so he could have peace.

The carriage rumbled through the night, first lurching over the frozen ruts of the mountain roads, then clattering over the cobblestones of the town's paved streets.

Eva folded her hands around the tarnished little token that belonged to the strange man at the monastery. She feigned a calmness she did not feel.

She had left Castle Frankenstein with nothing but the clothes she wore, and the token. Nothing belonged to her, nothing but the token. She dressed, she ate, she lived at the whim of Charles Frankenstein. From being the instrument of opening life to her, he had turned to a force for shutting her off from new experiences. When she chafed, he laughed. When she objected, he denied what he was doing. He had introduced her to freedom, then thoughtlessly and casually snatched it away.

She had admired him more than anyone she had ever met, above all the scintillating people at all the fashionable parties and balls. He had achieved so much, his intellect towered so far above all others, that she could hardly be surprised if he became impatient with her, if he no longer cared to be bothered by her. Eva doubted he would even notice she had left. From now on, she must be responsible for her own education and her own independence.

The driver halted the carriage. The team clattered and slid on the icy pavement. The coachman leaned over and opened the door. Eva stepped down to the street. She had never before noticed what a long step it was, because always before someone had placed small stairs by which she could descend; always before, someone had handed her down. The first time she rode in a carriage, she thought the custom strange and unnecessary; then she ceased to think about it at all; and finally she had come to expect it. Now, feeling clumsy for the lack of any help, she realized that the custom *was* strange—and, in an equally strange way, quite necessary indeed. It was one of the thousand tiny elements that made up her life, that made up the life of all women of her station. It was intended to convince her that she was so weak and helpless that she required it.

She slammed the coach door, lifted her skirts high, and strode to Josef Schildman's doorstep.

His manservant bowed her inside and took her to Josef's sitting room. He rose from his chair by the fire, one eyebrow arched as if he were surprised to see her, despite his invitation, despite his sending his coach in response to her message.

"Eva, what— Frankenstein—"

"I have left the Baron's house," she said. She took off her cloak and dropped it on the floor.

"When you said you would do as you pleased, I hardly thought—"

"Please don't speak," she said. She could barely speak, herself, for her heart pounded wildly with excitement and apprehension. "Please don't speak. I want to make love with you."

He stared at her for a moment, as if stunned. Then he crossed the space between them in two strides. He grasped her hand and kissed it. She remembered something she thought she had dreamed. She took his hand, turned it over, and kissed the palm, touching it lightly with her tongue. If she had dreamed it, why did she remember so clearly the smooth narrow ridges of a palm print, the faint salty taste on her tongue?

Josef shivered, pulled her to him, and kissed her lips very gently. She had seen people kiss; she had wondered how being kissed would feel.

He kissed her again. His lips parted and his tongue touched her mouth. She gasped in surprise and drew away.

"Oh!" she said. "I didn't know—"

He laughed softly, whispered "Shhh," and kissed her throat. She slid her hands up his back, and pulled him close. He breathed in her ear. He took the pins from her hair and let it fall curling around her shoulders. His breathing quickened. He picked her up, carried her to his bed, and laid her upon it. He knelt beside her, still kissing her. She stroked his hair, his face. He shrugged his open-collared shirt from his shoulders, and Eva drew it down his body, unbuttoning the last few buttons. It draped down around his hips. She had never seen a man with his shirt off before. She touched the dark hair on his chest. He bent close over her, opening her bodice, kissing her throat, her shoulders, her breasts, each inch of her as he bared it. She felt transported by his touch, she wanted it to go on forever, yet she wanted to discover if she had the power to give him such pleasure in return.

The light of the fire shifted, as if to caress them with brightness and shadows.

Suddenly, impossibly, Eva heard the sharp slash of braided leather cutting air, the heavier, uglier snap of leather against flesh. Josef shouted with shock and pain and leaped to his feet.

Silhouetted by the fire, Charles stood before them. He was pale with fury, his dilated eyes empty of anything but anger and his hand still clenched around his riding whip. He glared at Josef.

Josef calmly raised his hand to his cheek. A whip welt cut him from ear to chin. His fingers came away bloody.

"I will have satisfaction for this!" Charles cried.

Confused by Charles's anger, horrified by his violence, Eva sat up.

Josef wiped his bloody fingers on his shirt. His shoulders lifted then fell in a slight shrug.

"As you like, sir," he said. "You may even choose the weapons. I am equally skilled at all of them."

Charles pushed past him, grabbed Eva's arm, and jerked her to her feet.

"Put your clothes on, you little whore!" he snarled.

Eva felt like someone in a terrible nightmare, someone experiencing the events yet observing them from a distance. She tried to pull her bodice closed, for Charles had made her ashamed to be half naked in front of him and Josef.

Why does he have the right to make me feel ashamed? Eva thought, and her anger rose. Why does he have the right to speak to me in so ugly a way, with such ugly words? To break in here and tell me what I may or may not do? I will tell him—

But Josef spoke before she could tell Charles anything.

"If it makes any difference to you, Frankenstein," Josef said wearily, "the girl means nothing to me. She threw herself at me, so naturally I assumed you and she . . ." He shrugged again. "I had no idea your interests were concerned. So I took up the challenge. I am, after all . . . a man." There was no love in his voice, no regard, merely contempt.

Eva stared at him, astonished, as he smiled at Charles in an understanding way. Without a word or a look, he grasped Eva's arm and shoved her gently toward Charles.

Eva jerked herself away from him, away from Charles.

"Get away from me!" she cried. "Get away from me, both of you!"

Eva would rather have run out into the darkness and the snow, away from both men who had betrayed her. But Josef and Charles wrapped her in her cloak and hurried her downstairs, apparently having abandoned their quarrel with each other in order to ally themselves against her. Then Charles and his driver bundled her into the carriage. Charles sat across from her, still clutching his riding crop. Eva, infuriated, glared at him, but he would not meet her gaze. So she sat straight and angry, humiliated and confused, with her hands clenched in her cloak, until they returned to Castle Frankenstein.

Charles did not speak till they were behind the closed doors of the library. He stood before the hearth, with the fire spreading angry red light across his pale face. Struggling to master his emotions, he swung about to confront her.

"How could you do this!" he cried.

"What have I done that's so wrong?" Eva asked. "Charles, why are you angry at me?"

"Why! *Why?* You make love to that . . . that moronic dolt, and you ask me why I'm angry?"

"Are you angry because he is foolish? It's true, he hasn't your intellect. But you were bored with me, and he was not. He seemed sweet, and decent—" He no longer seemed so to her now, after his outburst, after he denied having any regard for her at all; but her opinion of Charles had changed, too, and just as radically.

"Sweet!" Charles shouted. "Decent!"

"Did you know he was not what he seemed? Could you not have told me?"

"He's a liar and a roué," Charles said, "and I should have known he wouldn't stop at ruining servant girls—I should have known he'd go so far as betraying me!"

"Why is this between you and him?" Eva asked. "Has it nothing to do with me—with what I want?"

He seemed not to hear her. "I cannot believe *you* would do this—to *me!*" he cried.

"To *you?* What has it got to do with you? A woman

should do as she pleases—just like a man. You taught me that."

"It's different with us, Eva," he said intensely. "We belong to each other."

"I don't belong to you!" Eva said, shocked. "You don't own me, like a mare!" He tried to interrupt her, but she refused to be intimidated or stopped. She must finally break away from Charles. "You taught me many things," she said more gently, trying to make him understand. "You fed me and clothed me. But I can make my own way, now. I can pay you back."

He sneered, his ugly, laughing sneer. "Make your own way! You have no skills with which to make your way—not even the one you tried to learn tonight! As for paying me back—for a lifetime of work and experience? I think not."

"I am leaving here."

"You are not. Not alone—and not with anyone else." He shook his head, and said patiently, as if to a child, "There are some things you don't understand, Eva."

"What 'things'?" she asked belligerently.

"It's enough that I tell you they exist. You must trust me for the present. And you must obey me."

"I will not obey you! I will not!"

"Don't provoke me, Eva," he said, his voice rising again.

"I will provoke you! You lied to me about who I am—there was no girl found near Brucor! You lied about everything!"

"You insult me—and I will not have it."

"*You* won't have it! You lied to me—and *you* are insulted? Who do you think you are?"

Charles looked so angry that for a moment Eva thought he would try to strike her. But he calmed abruptly, rocked back on his heels, folded his arms across his chest, and smiled.

"If you go on like this," he said, "I shall have to tell you."

He spoke with a hint of menace, yet also with anticipation, and Eva took up the challenge.

"Tell me, then! I have a life of my own! You taught me, out of books—but you didn't *create* me! You didn't create *me!*"

He laughed. Charles Frankenstein seldom laughed. The sound chilled Eva more deeply than the coldest of winds.

"As a matter of fact, my dear," he said, savoring each word, "I did."

Eva stared at him, uncomprehending.

"I sewed you together out of corpses, and brought you to life by means of an electrical charge. I created your body just as I created your mind." He moved toward her, looking down triumphantly. "And I can uncreate it, too."

Eva shook her head. She dared not speak; what he said could not be true, and he must be mad.

"You wanted the truth, my dear," Charles said, "and there you have it. I hope it pleases you."

"I don't believe it," she whispered. "I don't know what you're talking about."

"No? Then you soon will."

He took her by the arm. She was too stunned to resist, too stunned, too afraid—for herself and for him.

He led her to the mirror, where he paused and gazed at their reflection for a moment. His reflection touched its neck-cloth and pushed its hair from its forehead. Then it reached toward them. The reflection of the silvered glass seemed so clear and magically real that Eva flinched back, startled, from the grasping hand. Charles chuckled and tightened his grip on her arm.

"What, my dear, frightened?"

He touched the mirror and it slid open. Beyond it lay a secret room, filled with strange instruments and intricate toys, redolent with a heavy, vaguely familiar odor. Charles struck a match and lit a massive black candle that reflected into infinity from a triptych of mirrors behind it. Eva had never suspected the chamber's existence.

Charles took several notebooks from a high shelf. He stroked one finger across their singed, water-stained covers.

"These are my journals," he said. "They are records of certain . . . experiments. You may find them instructive."

He snuffed out the candle and strode from the room, leaving Eva to gaze about her for a moment, trying to understand how so much about Frankenstein could have been so obscure to her.

Without another word, Frankenstein tossed the three journals onto the table and left the library. The door closed firmly behind him.

Eva emerged from the secret chamber and hesitated with her hand on the sooty cover of one of the journals. The mirror slid shut behind her. The mirror shut the secret room away and cut off the source of the soporific odor. Eva smelled the burned-paper scent of Charles's journals.

She sat down at the library table.

She clenched her hand to still its trembling, picked up the notebooks, and started to read.

Charles strolled down the corridor to the great hall, chuckling. He had taught Eva a lesson; he had taught her her place. When she finished reading his laboratory records, she would never defy him again.

He threw himself into a chair before the fire, sprawling out before the hearth to let the warmth soak into his chilled body. He had driven to Josef Schildman's house in a fever of rage and apprehension, and back home again in a state of cold anger that froze him to the heart.

He wanted a pipe of opium, but he did not want to return

to his secret room. He wanted Eva to sit in the library all alone for every minute of the time it took her to read the notebooks.

Charles cursed loudly and reached for the cut-glass decanter.

He poured brandy into a large snifter and drank it in a gulp. He smiled sardonically: he knew what Clerval would say to treating good cognac in such a manner. But he was sick of Clerval and all his misbegotten friends, particularly Herr Colonel Schildman. They would surely be laughing at Charles by morning.

Charles poured another glass of brandy; again he drank it in a gulp.

He did not care what they thought.

Chapter 13

Eva followed Charles's spidery handwriting through a story she wished she could refuse to believe.

"I could not salvage the hands of the corpse. I must graft new ones onto the existing limbs. . . ."

Eva let the journal fall into her lap and grasped her own wrists. The scars existed: she knew that quite well. Nevertheless, she looked at them again: thread-thin, almost imperceptible lines. At least she knew now that she did not, in the time before she could remember, try to commit suicide.

Or perhaps I did, she thought. And perhaps . . . I succeeded.

Her eyes filled with tears; the magnitude of what she had learned and what still remained to be known struck her like a blow.

Charles started from a deep, drunken sleep. The light of the coals failed to push the darkness from the hall.

Was that a scream that had awakened him? He believed it was, and he smiled cruelly. Now Eva must know how completely he held her in his power.

She strode silently out of the blackness, clutching the notebooks. Without a word, she flung them into the fireplace. They agitated the coals, and soon a fringe of fire licked at the pages, curled them, blackened them, and exploded them into flame. The light glistened from the tears on Eva's cheeks.

"Why are you weeping, my dear?" Charles asked, his voice silky. "Your mystery is solved. You have what you want—you ought to be happy."

"Where is he?" Eva asked abruptly.

Charles stared blankly at her. She should be begging his forgiveness and his mercy, vowing her gratitude—and here she was questioning him in her defiant tone, the light in her eyes more excitement than fear.

"Where is who?" Charles said.

"The other being—the 'creature'—you made me for."

"He perished in the tower fire—I'm happy to say," Charles said.

Eva turned away with a sob. "Then I'm alone," she said, so softly he could barely hear her. "There is no one else in the world like me."

"You miss the point, my dear," Charles said. "It's true I made you because that . . . that abortion demanded a friend. But I quickly saw the foolishness of that. You're fit for better things."

She faced him again, glaring belligerently. "What do you mean by that?"

"I taught you a great deal, Eva. I made you my equal in thought and reasoning. I gave you the gift of freedom. Intellectual freedom. But you didn't trust me. You tried to progress beyond the level for which I had prepared you." He shook his head sadly. "You should not have been so impatient. You cannot learn love by yourself. Love was the last thing I planned to teach you, and you nearly jumped the gun. But I found you in time, didn't I?"

He stood up and moved toward her, savoring her beauty and allure. She stepped back and thrust him away. She was trembling, and this excited him.

"Stay away from me!"

He could hear the urgency and the terror in her voice. He

pressed his advantage till Eva could move no farther, till his presence bent her back against the sofa.

"You forget," Charles said. "I made you out of ashes. Ashes and dust. I can always reduce you to ashes and start again."

She slid quickly sideways, momentarily escaping him.

"You can do what you like!" she said. "You can take apart the body you put together, and you can take away the life you gave me. But you cannot have *me*. Not ever. Not if you murdered me and raised me up a thousand times. You cannot have *me!*"

For a moment he was caught by her preternatural eyes, and he could only admire the Promethean rebelliousness of her spirit. But with the grudging admiration came envy, and the realization that while she had the right to defy any other being in the world, she did not have the right to defy *him*, Baron Charles Frankenstein, her creator.

"I made you for a wedding, my dear," he said. "And your wedding night has come 'round at last."

He grabbed her wrist and jerked her toward him. Eva cried out with surprise and anger, twisted away, and fled.

Charles pursued her down the corridor and through the entrance hall. She dragged back the bolt. If she eluded him long enough to reach the stables, long enough to reach one of the horses, she would flee into the night and escape him forever. As she flung open the massive door, he lunged toward her, reached past her, and slammed it shut again. Infuriated by her attempt to escape him, he grabbed her shoulder. She flinched away from him. He clutched at the fabric of her dress and it tore in his hand. She screamed and struck at him, terrified and humiliated.

Viktor started from a state half dream, half unconsciousness. He thought he had heard a cry of despair, a cry for help. He looked around desperately. Now that he was awake he heard only the stones, whispering of suffering and pain, and the rats, rustling through the dirty straw on the floor of the prison cell. Soon the stones would add his whispers to their lament, and the rats of a potter's field would gnaw his bones.

But he could not drift back into his dreams, where Rinaldo still lived and Viktor still hoped to make the new being his friend. A strange and silent force drew him, frightening him out of his resignation.

He twisted his hands, testing the iron shackles.

Charles let Eva go, shocked that she would continue to defy him. They stared at each other. Eva looked at him as if she had never seen him before.

She ran from him. Charles slammed home the bolt and chased her into the library. He let his fury at her defiance propel him, for his shock at her behavior made him dizzy and faint.

He trapped her in the library, as if she were a vixen and he a hound. He circled toward her, but she kept the study table between them. Suddenly she grabbed a book from the shelf and threw it at him. He warded it off with his forearm, but it struck him hard. He stepped back and protected himself with a chair as Eva flung more books.

He laughed.

"And what will you do when you run out of books?" he said. "You're only postponing the inevitable. It's love, or death. You can choose."

In desperation, she tried to flee past him again. He grabbed her, spun her around, and slapped her across the face.

"It is no choice!" she cried. "Your 'love' is no love—"

"You force me to do this, Eva," he said. A thick drop of

blood spilled from her cut lip and streaked her chin with scarlet. He slapped her again.

Viktor felt the blow; he experienced the confusion and terror and despair as if it were his own. He strained against the shackles. They gave, first almost imperceptibly, then bursting and ripping from the wall all of a sudden. He kicked his feet free, strode two paces to the door, and smashed it down.

Flushed with excitement, Charles pressed Eva back against the library table. She trembled with the effort of holding him away. He knew she would cease her struggling once he had kissed her. He leaned closer, aroused by her resistance.

Suddenly she kicked him hard in the shin. He shouted in pain and his grip loosened just long enough for her to slip sideways, leaving him panting and groaning against the table. He forced himself to his feet again. He stumbled after her. She ran up the staircase. He followed, but as he reached the head of the stairs, the door of her room slammed shut and the lock clicked to.

He paused outside her door.

"Eva, let me in."

She remained silent.

"You are forcing me to drastic action, my dear."

He tried the door, but it remained solidly fastened. He rubbed his chin, considering. The heavy door would be difficult to break down; besides, he had no need to exert himself so strenuously. She could not escape him now. Chuckling, he sauntered away.

Exhausted by their pursuit of Viktor and made drowsy by their celebratory libations, the guards of the dungeon snored softly at their posts. They did not stir when Viktor passed.

The streets were deserted. The townspeople had gathered in a nearby tavern to rejoice over Viktor's capture. He could hear them from a block away.

The only creatures to notice his presence were the saddle horses tethered across the street. They scented him; they snorted and shifted nervously. But a mood of desperation possessed Viktor. He crossed the street. The largest horse pulled away and strained at its tied reins as Viktor approached. White showed all around its eyes, its nostrils flared, and it flattened its ears against its head. Viktor loosened the reins, trying not to appear frightened. Wild-eyed, the horse backed up several steps, then stood trembling and blowing at the limits of the reins.

Viktor stretched out his hand slowly, gently. The horse's ears flicked forward. He touched the horse's muzzle. He came close enough to blow into its nostrils.

"Help me," he whispered. He touched the horse's smooth shoulder. Its trembling ceased, and Viktor himself felt less afraid. He grasped the horse's mane and vaulted to its back.

Before he fairly got his seat, the horse sprang into a gallop and clattered down the street. Viktor held on for dear life.

Eva stood with her back to the door, leaning against it, as if she could somehow keep Charles from breaking it down. In confusion and despair she pressed her hands, fingers spread, against the silken wood. She sought an instant of stability and calm in the midst of a world disintegrating around her. Could it be that she, as Charles claimed, was responsible for his violence? She tried to understand how that was possible. He had taught her about freedom, but when she accepted the gift, he tried to snatch it back from her. She did not comprehend a freedom to do only what another permitted.

She took a deep, gasping breath and squeezed her eyes shut. All the pleasant memories of Charles seemed very far away; they seemed like stories she had heard of some other person, a long, long time ago. She opened her eyes again and looked around the room. All the furniture was either too fragile to use as a blockade, or too heavy for one person alone to move.

Since she could not block the door, she must either escape or defend herself. She ran to the window and flung it open. She leaned out and felt in the darkness for the ivy that twined up the wall.

It was gone. All around her windows the ivy had been ripped away, leaving a clear space of stone and no vine within her reach.

She went to her dressing table and picked up the longest hat pin in her jewelry case.

She carried it with her to the darkest corner of her room, hid herself there, and there she waited.

Charles entered his secret room, filled a pipe with opium, lit it, and drew the heavy smoke deep into his lungs. He exhaled with a sigh of relief. The drug steadied him immediately. The brandy he had drunk fueled his anger; the opium refined it. Everything Eva was, he had made her. It was one thing for her to outrage and fascinate polite society by defending her opinions in the face of her betters and her elders; it was one thing for her to shock the otherwise imperturbable William Clerval. But it was quite another for her to defy Charles Frankenstein. Perhaps William, with his cynical attitude, had been right all along.

Charles found the keys to the upper floor and took the stairs two at a time. He rapped on Eva's door.

"Eva! If you do not open the door, you will force me to teach you a lesson you'll not soon forget."

She made no reply. He sighed; but perhaps it was better that she learn obedience now. Clearly, that was the important lesson he needed to teach her.

Eva heard the key turn in the lock. She tightened her grasp on the hat pin. The door crashed open and Charles strode in, deathly pale, his eyes black, smiling maniacally.

He stopped when he saw the hat pin, and the smile faded.

"You little bitch," he said. He grabbed a silver candlestick from her mantelpiece and advanced on her. He grinned, but the grin held no humor, only sarcasm. "Why, I should have brought my sabre," he said. "No wonder you harried me to teach you fencing, if we've come to this. Do you think you can best me in swordplay, my dear?" He advanced upon her, *en garde,* taunting and teasing her.

She knew that she could not best him in swordplay, for she had never raised her hand against anyone in anger. William Clerval's assertion that a gentleman would always be nearby, to relieve her of the responsibility of self-defense, now seemed empty and perverted.

She would not give up. She lunged at Frankenstein. The hat pin raked a long cut in his hand and the blood welled out. He screamed in pain and rage and struck out with the candlestick. The heavy base crashed down on her shoulder. She staggered. Frankenstein tripped her and she fell, landing so hard the breath left her. Instantly he stamped his boot onto her scarred wrist, crushing her half-crippled arm against the floor until, though she struggled and clawed at him with her free hand, the pin slipped from her numb, trapped fingers. The jeweled head of the pin clattered against the floor. Droplets of blood from his slashed hand spattered her arm.

Wrenching her injured shoulder till she gasped in pain, he

dragged her to her feet and struck her again, slapping the side of her face, then her temple. Her head snapped back with the force of the blow. Her vision blurred. She could feel nothing of her body but the pain of her shoulder, her wrist, her temple. She fought to retain her awareness.

"Now we will see who's master of this house."

She flinched from his nearness, from his triumphant shout. He flung her onto the bed.

He turned away long enough to lock her door and pocket the key. As he came toward her again she struggled up, sobbing for breath, and clawed at his eyes. Cursing, he backhanded her across the cheek and temple.

The clatter of hooves in the courtyard did not even cause him to hesitate. He flung a sheet at her, twisting and tangling her arms in it. She felt his fingers at her breast, heard the tearing as he ripped her dress again, felt the cold air on her body. He bent over her, and she saw his eyes.

She screamed. She screamed. She heard the crash of broken timber from downstairs, but she no longer hoped for help from any human agency. Humans preyed on each other, and none would feel sympathy for her. But she screamed, and struggled desperately, fighting for her life. For she had seen into his eyes, and she knew now that whatever happened, whether she submitted or he forced her to obey him, Frankenstein intended to return her to the dust and ashes.

Suddenly the door of her room exploded from its hinges. Splinters and shards of wood clattered across the floor. Frankenstein glanced away from Eva for an instant, then, with a violent oath, he flung her viciously against the headboard of her bed.

The last thing she saw, as she lost her tenuous hold on consciousness, was a tall, shadowed figure standing in the shattered doorway.

As Viktor pulled the last dangling plank from its hinges, the soundless summons of despair faded and died. Frankenstein turned toward him. Blood covered the Baron's hands.

The new being, Viktor's friend, lay unmoving on the bed.

"You!" Frankenstein cried.

Ignoring the Baron, Viktor moaned with grief. He was too late. Just as he had been too late to save Rinaldo, he was too late to save *her*. He gazed at her, willing her to rise.

Suddenly Frankenstein appeared again before him, gripping a flaming brand from the hearth.

"I'm not afraid of you!" he said. "Even if you are a ghost. And if you're not, I'll finish the job properly this time."

He jabbed at Viktor's face. Viktor slapped uselessly at the fire, fear and grief sapping him of strength.

"You always were afraid of fire, weren't you!" Frankenstein said. He jabbed at Viktor again. "Now you have cause to be afraid, sir!"

He snatched up a lamp, sent the mantle crashing to the floor, and flung the oil at Viktor. It splashed over his face and clothes, warm and pungent. Viktor lurched away from the fire in Frankenstein's hand. The heat terrified him. Frankenstein lunged at him, striking his arm with the burning stick. The oil on his ragged shirt burst into flame. Viktor whimpered and beat his arm against the wall. Frankenstein laughed and poked the stick at him again.

Pursued by the fire, by the Baron's triumphant chuckle, Viktor fled.

He ran down a dark corridor, lost in the maze of the castle. The hallway branched abruptly to the right and left. Viktor heard Frankenstein's footsteps behind him; he saw his own shadow, cast by the flickering light of the torch. He turned down the darkest passage.

The passage led deeper and deeper into the castle, turning and twisting. Finally it led into a small chamber, a small chamber with one walled-up doorway and no other exits but the one by which he had entered.

He recognized the chamber. It was the place where Frankenstein and Zahlus had sat, making their plans to give Viktor life, and to make it a life of suffering.

He saw the flickering light of the torch; he smelled the burning resin and heard the sizzle of pitch. Frankenstein entered, hunting him, supreme in his confidence and power.

Viktor's moan of sorrow and weariness filled the chamber. He flung himself away from the burning torch, straight into the mortared wall.

The surface cracked before him, and he smashed into it again. It collapsed completely, shattering away in a rain of rock and earth-scented limestone. Viktor fled.

He had no choice. He must climb to the tower. He had no thought but to escape the fire.

But at the head of the stairs, he stopped. The ruins of his birthplace lay around him: the broken table, the shattered generator, the dangling wires that reached into the sky to give him life. Every surface glittered with frost. The ice crystals sparkled in the moonlight, chill and white, as beautiful as jewels, but not as beautiful as she whom he had first seen here. He had seen her beginning and he had seen her end, and now he wished for nothing but an end to his own suffering. He sought no revenge. He had taken his revenge for Rinaldo's death. It had gained him nothing, not even peace.

The light turned scarlet as Frankenstein burst into the destruction of the laboratory. Viktor fled, climbing to the battlements.

"You won't escape me again!" Frankenstein cried. "Not now!"

Viktor reached the top of the tower. He wished for darkness, but the frost and the rainbow-ringed moon lit the night with an eerie pallor. Viktor circled the gap in the roof of the tower. He looked over the edge. The sheer cliff fell two hundred feet to shattered rocks. The earth's teeth so far below would tear the life from him quickly, and much less painfully than the death by fire that Frankenstein planned for him.

The Baron emerged onto the top of the tower, flailing his torch before him, the glint of triumph and madness in his eyes. His torch blazed brightly. He circled the battlements. Viktor stepped onto the icy surface of the parapet. He took a deep breath. The smell of smoke and burning pitch tinged the cold air.

As if sensing his intention, as if unwilling to permit him a choice even in his own death, Frankenstein sprang toward him, thrusting with the blazing torch.

Suddenly the Baron's foot slipped on the frost-slick stone and his torch spun away. Stumbling, he flung out his hands to regain his balance. But the explosion of his laboratory had weakened the structure of the tower, and the parapet crumbled beneath him.

He fell.

His scream ended in a terrible crushing sound.

Viktor climbed shakily from the parapet and looked over its edge.

Baron Charles Frankenstein lay crumpled at the foot of the cliff. He moved feebly. His head fell back and he gazed up blankly. Whether he could see Viktor, or the rainbow around the moon, or only darkness, Viktor never knew. The Baron collapsed, and did not move again.

The torch blazed brightly beside him.

Viktor did not want a death like that.

Cries echoed faintly in the distance. Viktor saw a patch of light on the road leading from the town to Castle Frankenstein. He made out a group of people carrying torches and lanterns, coming this way. Someone had observed Viktor's flight and sounded the alarm.

He hurried down the stairs, passed through the broken laboratory without another glance, and made his way out of the castle's ruined tower.

At the new being's room, he paused.

He entered her chamber to bid her a final farewell.

She was breathing.

Surprise and joy made him gasp. Her face was bloody and bruised, her clothes torn, but she was alive and she was breathing regularly, strongly.

The shouts of the townspeople echoed ever closer.

Viktor reached out, but he stayed his hand before he touched her. He was afraid she might wake and remember the first time she woke, the first time she saw him. Better that she should remember him as an itinerant beggar, seen once, befriended, pitied.

He tucked the bedclothes around her to keep her from the cold. A moment later, he fled into the night.

Eva woke slowly from a dream. She had never expected to wake at all. Darkness surrounded her. She rose. The comforter slid from her; the chill air flowed over her. Who had drawn the comforter around her? Not Frankenstein, surely.

Utter silence filled the castle.

Eva wrapped herself in the comforter and stole cautiously into the hall. Perhaps Frankenstein merely meant to let her regain consciousness. She hurried down the stairs, planning to take his sabre from the wall of the library. Perhaps she did not know how to use it properly, but at least it would give her some advantage.

She heard voices.

She pressed herself into shadows, hiding, till she was certain the voices were echoes of people outside.

She hurried to a window and leaned over the deep sill.

At the bottom of the cliff, a mob of townspeople with clubs and torches stood in a circle.

"He's dead," one of them said. "Our benefactor—murdered by that fiend!"

"We'll capture the monster!"

"Vengeance!"

They trooped away, leaving behind tracks in the frost, the echoes of their angry cries . . .

. . . and the body of Charles Frankenstein.

Eva gasped. She remembered part of her dream: she remembered the shape in the doorway; she remembered the man at the monastery.

All at once she knew what had happened, and she knew the man from the monastery was in deadly danger. He had saved her, and now he would be killed if she let the mob catch him.

She flew back to her room.

The fire had died to gray ashes, leaving only moonlight to light the chamber. She flung off the torn dress and scrambled into her sturdiest riding habit. At her dressing table, she scooped her jewelry from its case and tied it into a handkerchief. She felt no more compunction about taking what technically belonged to Baron Frankenstein.

She kept back the tarnished gold chain with the gondola; that bit of jewelry, she put around her neck.

As she rose to go, she glanced into her mirror and started at the grotesque mask that peered back at her. Blood smeared her face, and tears streaked the blood. If anyone saw her they would think her a ghoul. Breaking the thin crust of ice on the water in the basin, she quickly scrubbed her face. Her lips were tender from the blows, and her ears rang, but the bruises had already faded.

Eva leaned close over the neck of her fierce gray mare and urged her faster through the silver light of dawn. A second horse galloped behind them. She could see the torches of the mob on the road above, but she could cut cross-country. She would arrive at the monastery before they could reach it. She did not even stop to think how she knew that the man she had first seen at the monastery would be there now.

Fog drifted through the old churchyard as the morning light melted the frost. Eva chose a route that took her to the back of the cemetery. She leaped from her horse and flung the reins over a tree branch, then climbed the wall.

She could hear angry voices echoing through the valley as the mob approached the monastery.

Only a few yards away the man huddled behind a gravestone, shivering with cold. Eva jumped down. The man spun toward her, starting with fear. Eva put her finger to her lips. He glanced back over his shoulder; he nodded at her: he understood.

She took the chain from around her throat and held it out to him.

"This has the name of Venice written on it. Would you like to go to Venice?"

He stared at her, disbelieving, but finally nodded again.

"Yes," he said. "The streets are made of water."

"I know." Suddenly, despite the danger of their position, despite the urgency, she felt quite shy. "When you gave this to me," she said hesitantly, "you looked at me—no one ever looked at me that way before, right into my heart. But you . . ."

"I . . ." He spoke with difficulty, in a voice soft and hoarse, yet not unpleasant. "I have a name!"

"What is it?"

"Viktor."

"That's a good name," Eva said. "It means: 'he will win.' "

Viktor stretched his hands toward her, pleading, desperate, then abruptly dropped his arms and stared at the ground.

Eva drew in a deep shuddering breath of comprehension. She remembered the rest of her dream: the shape in the doorway, the man at the monastery . . . and the events surrounding her own creation. She realized that she had known of this new being's peril the same way he had known of hers.

"Do you know who made you?" she asked.

"Yes," Viktor said reluctantly.

"Do you know who I am?"

He nodded. Without looking up, he whispered, "Yes. I know."

She hurried toward him; she grasped his hands and raised them, and her tears of joy and relief fell upon his weathered skin.

"Then you must tell me," she said. "You must tell me everything! And I—I have so much to tell you. The world is so big. It's so full of things, all waiting for us to see them. . . ."

He raised his head and looked into her eyes. She touched his hair, hardly able to believe that he existed, that they had found each other. She took his hand again, and his fingers closed gently around hers.

The shouts of the mob echoed closer.

"We have to go," Eva said. "We have to get out of here."

She led him toward the horses, toward the world that waited, toward freedom.

The more you know the man, the more you'll love his music

Lionel Richie

An imtimate biography with 16 pages of personal photos, *Lionel Richie* makes endlessly fascinating reading as it goes behind the headlines to the man himself—his childhood in Mississippi, his early days with the Commodores, his decision to go solo, his platinum-plus recordings, and his MTV video fame. Singer, songwriter, producer, and instrumentalist, Lionel Richie has given the old-fashioned love song a soulful new twist, making it *the* music of the 80s.

14851-0-10 $3.50

by Roberta Plutzik

At your local bookstore or use this handy coupon for ordering:

DELL READERS SERVICE-Dept. B661A
P.O. BOX 1000, PINE BROOK, N.J. 07058

Please send me the above title(s). I am enclosing $_____ (please add 75¢ per copy to cover postage and handling). Send check or money order—no cash or CODs. Please allow 3-4 weeks for shipment. <u>CANADIAN ORDERS</u>: please submit in U.S. dollars.

Ms./Mrs./Mr._____

Address_____

City/State_____ Zip _____

Snip it.
Shear it.
Dye it.
Riot.

From Mohawks to dreadlocks,
buzz-cuts, and beyond— a must-have
manual of hip hair fashion and techniques! Read it and
learn the step-by-step instructions for every punk style.
Preppies & Yuppies: find out how to look like an honor
student (or young executive) by day, and a video
vixen by night.

53660-X-13   **$3.95**

HIP HAIR

by SUSAN FLINKER
Photographs by DEBORAH FEINGOLD

At your local bookstore or use this handy coupon for ordering:

DELL READERS SERVICE-Dept. B661C
P.O. BOX 1000, PINE BROOK, N.J. 07058

Please send me the above title(s). I am enclosing $_____(please add 75¢ per copy to cover
postage and handling). Send check or money order--no cash or CODs. Please allow 3-4 weeks for shipment.
<u>CANADIAN ORDERS: please submit in U.S. dollars.</u>

Ms./Mrs./Mr._____

Address_____

City/State_____Zip _____